Toby and the Talking Train

Freya Jobe

Published by Freya Jobe, 2024.

This is a work of fiction. Similarities to real people, places, or events are entirely coincidental.

TOBY AND THE TALKING TRAIN

First edition. November 2, 2024.

Copyright © 2024 Freya Jobe.

ISBN: 979-8227906342

Written by Freya Jobe.

Toby and the Talking Train

In a small town nestled between rolling hills and whispering woods, lived a young boy named Toby. Toby was a curious soul, always exploring, always asking questions. But there was one place Toby was told never to go—the old railway tracks hidden deep in the woods. People said the tracks led nowhere and were abandoned long ago.

One crisp autumn afternoon, Toby's curiosity got the better of him. With a quick glance over his shoulder, he slipped away from the world he knew and into the trees. The forest was alive with mystery, the air thick with leaves and the scent of adventure. Just as he was about to turn back, he heard something unusual—a faint whistle echoing through the trees. Following the sound, he stumbled upon an old train, covered in vines and rust, as if it had been waiting for him all this time.

To Toby's astonishment, the train was no ordinary train. Its name was Whistle, and it could talk.

Whistle wasn't just any train; it had stories to tell, secrets to share, and adventures to take Toby on. Together, they would journey through magical forests, visit hidden valleys, and travel through time itself. But more than that, Whistle would teach Toby lessons about kindness, courage, and the magic that lives inside each of us.

This is the story of Toby and the Talking Train, an unforgettable friendship that would stay with Toby forever.

Let the journey begin!

Chapter 1: The Train Station Discovery

Toby loved to explore. On weekends, he'd dart out of his house right after breakfast, already dreaming of the adventures he might find. There were fields and forests around his home, places that were familiar but always held something new if he looked closely enough. But today felt different. Toby had a strange feeling he couldn't shake, a little like excitement but also like a secret waiting to be discovered. He decided to follow his curiosity and head into the forest, deeper than he had ever gone before.

The morning sun filtered through the trees, casting long beams of light across the ground, lighting up the fallen leaves in shades of gold and amber. He walked slowly, listening to the rustling sounds of small animals in the undergrowth and the occasional chirp of a bird. The deeper he went, the quieter the forest became, as if the trees were holding their breath.

After a while, Toby noticed something unusual. Ahead of him, partially hidden under a thick carpet of leaves and twigs, was a line of rusty metal. He crouched down to get a better look, brushing aside the dirt. His heart raced as he realized he was staring at a pair of old train tracks, their metal rails worn and bent slightly, as though they hadn't been used for years. Toby stood up, looking around. Why were there train tracks here in the middle of the forest? He hadn't seen them before, even though he'd explored this part of the woods many times.

Curiosity got the better of him, and he decided to follow the tracks, brushing his hand along the rough metal as he walked. The tracks led him farther and farther into the trees, winding through the undergrowth and twisting around thick trunks. He felt like he was being pulled forward, almost as if the tracks were guiding him somewhere special, somewhere forgotten.

After walking for what felt like a long time, Toby noticed a clearing up ahead. Stepping into it, he gasped. There, hidden in a nest of overgrown bushes and ivy, was an old, abandoned train station. It was a small building, weathered and faded, with bricks that had long since lost their color. Vines clung to the walls, and the roof was partially caved in. Above the door, barely visible through the layers of dust and grime, was a wooden sign that read Willow Creek Station.

Toby took a step closer, drawn to the station's quiet mystery. He could almost feel the echoes of the past clinging to the air, as if the station had stories waiting to be told. He imagined people bustling about, tickets in hand, waiting for trains that would take them on grand adventures. But now, it was silent, a place forgotten by time.

As he moved around the platform, something else caught his eye. At the edge of the station, half-hidden by shadows, stood a train. It was an old engine, with a long line of carriages stretching back into the trees. The train's paint was chipped and faded, but Toby could still make out hints of deep green and bright red. He stepped closer, feeling a strange pull toward it.

On the side of the engine, written in curly, gold letters, was a name: Whistle. Toby reached out and touched the letters, feeling the cool metal under his fingertips. It was strange, standing beside something so still and silent. The train seemed lonely, as if it had been waiting for someone to find it. He imagined it had once been a proud, gleaming train, carrying passengers to far-off places, the sound of its whistle echoing through the trees. Now, it sat quietly, its windows clouded with dust, its wheels rusted and unmoving.

Toby walked along the length of the train, peering into the windows. Inside, he could see rows of empty seats, all covered in a fine layer of dust. The seats were upholstered in green fabric, though time had dulled their color. Everything was frozen in place, like a snapshot of a different era. There were old luggage racks overhead, some with forgotten bags still resting in them. He tried the door handle, but it was stuck fast, as though the train were holding onto its secrets.

A soft breeze drifted through the clearing, and for a moment, Toby thought he heard a faint whistling sound. He stopped, listening intently, but the sound faded away, leaving only the quiet rustling of leaves. He shook his head, wondering if his imagination was playing tricks on him. After all, it wasn't every day you stumbled upon an abandoned train hidden in the forest.

He walked back to the front of the train, sitting down on the edge of the platform. He gazed at the engine, letting his thoughts wander. He imagined what it would be like to climb into the driver's seat, to pull on the levers and hear the train roar to life. He could almost picture it—the trees flying past as Whistle rumbled down the tracks, its whistle cutting through the air, a sound both thrilling and comforting.

Lost in his daydream, Toby reached out and placed his hand on the side of the engine, giving it a gentle pat. For a moment, he felt a strange warmth under his hand, a pulse of energy that vanished almost as quickly as it appeared. He pulled his hand back, staring at the spot where he'd touched the train. It was odd, but it made him feel strangely connected to Whistle, as if he'd found a friend in this silent, forgotten train.

As he sat there, he wondered why no one had ever mentioned this place. It seemed like something people would talk about—a hidden station, an abandoned train. But whenever he'd asked his parents or his friends about the woods, they only ever mentioned the usual things: the big oak tree, the stream where he liked to fish, the clearing where wildflowers bloomed in the spring. No one had ever said anything about Willow Creek Station or Whistle.

Toby thought about telling his parents about the train, but something made him hesitate. This felt like his own secret, something magical and mysterious, just for him. He liked the idea of coming back here whenever he wanted, of sitting beside Whistle and imagining all the adventures they could have. It was almost as if the train had been waiting for him, as if it had been lonely and forgotten for so long that it needed someone like Toby to bring it back to life.

The sun began to sink lower in the sky, casting long shadows across the clearing. Toby knew he should head home before it got too dark, but he felt reluctant to leave. He stood up, brushing the dust from his pants, and took one last look at the train. In the soft glow of the late afternoon sun, Whistle looked almost alive, as if it were watching him, waiting.

Before he turned to leave, he placed his hand on the side of the train one last time. "I'll be back," he whispered, feeling a surge of excitement at the thought. It was a promise, a secret pact between him and Whistle. With a final glance, he stepped off the platform and started back along the tracks, casting one last look over his shoulder as the train faded into the shadows.

As he walked through the forest, he thought he heard the faintest sound of a whistle, a soft, distant note that made the hairs on the back of his neck stand up. He stopped, listening, but the sound disappeared, leaving only the gentle rustling of leaves in its place. He shook his head, smiling to himself. Maybe it was just the wind, or maybe it was Whistle saying goodbye.

That night, as Toby lay in bed, he couldn't stop thinking about the train. He wondered where it had come from, who had ridden it, and why it had been left behind. But more than that, he felt a strange, comforting sense of belonging, as if he'd found a place meant just for him.

In his dreams, he was standing beside Whistle, the forest alive with color and light, the train's whistle echoing through the trees. He climbed into the driver's seat, his hands on the levers, ready to set off on an adventure unlike any he'd ever known.

And as he drifted deeper into sleep, he could almost feel the ground rumble beneath him, the wheels turning, the train coming to life.

Chapter 2: The First Conversation

The next morning, Toby woke up with a strange, persistent sense of excitement. The memory of the hidden station and the old train lingered in his mind like a half-remembered dream, yet he knew it had been real. Whistle was out there, waiting in the woods, and for reasons he couldn't explain, Toby felt compelled to go back. He skipped breakfast, tossing a quick "I'll be back soon!" to his mom before darting out the door and heading toward the forest.

The air was crisp, and a soft mist hung around the trees as he made his way back to the secret tracks. The leaves under his feet were damp and smelled faintly of earth. He followed the line of rusty metal rails, winding through the trees until the clearing came into view. His heart leapt when he saw Whistle, just as he had left it, sitting silently at the platform of Willow Creek Station.

Toby approached slowly, feeling the same strange connection he'd felt the day before. The train looked so still, so lonely, but somehow welcoming, as if it had been waiting for him all along.

"Hi, Whistle," he murmured softly, feeling a little silly talking to an old train. But as soon as the words left his mouth, something strange happened. The air around him seemed to thrum with energy, and for a moment, he thought he heard a faint whisper, almost like a sigh, coming from the train.

He froze, staring at the engine. Had he really heard something, or was it just his imagination? He took a cautious step closer and placed his hand on Whistle's side. The metal was cold and smooth, but beneath it, he could feel a faint vibration, a steady, pulsing rhythm like a heartbeat.

"Hello, Toby."

Toby jerked his hand back, eyes wide. The voice was soft, barely more than a whisper, but it was unmistakably real. He stared at the train, his heart pounding, hardly daring to breathe.

"Did you... did you just talk?" he asked, his voice trembling with a mixture of awe and disbelief.

There was a pause, and then the voice spoke again, a little louder this time. "Yes, I did. I've been waiting for someone to find me."

Toby's mouth dropped open. He could hardly believe what he was hearing. An old train, hidden away in the forest, abandoned and covered in dust... and it could talk? He glanced around, half-expecting someone to jump out and yell "Surprise!" but the clearing was empty, silent except for the soft, low voice coming from the train.

"What... how... I mean, how are you talking?" Toby stammered, trying to make sense of what was happening.

The train let out a gentle hum, almost like a chuckle. "It's a bit of a long story," Whistle replied. "But I suppose you could say I've always had a voice. Only, no one's been around to listen for a very long time."

Toby's eyes sparkled with wonder as he took in Whistle's words. It was as if he'd stepped into one of his favourite storybooks, where trains could talk and adventures waited around every corner. The forest seemed alive with magic, and Whistle was at the heart of it.

"So... you've been here all this time, just waiting?" Toby asked, his voice filled with curiosity.

"Yes," Whistle said softly. "I used to carry passengers all across the land, people from all walks of life. We went to cities, mountains, valleys... you name it. I knew every station, every turn in the tracks. But one day, my journey stopped. People stopped riding, and I was left here, forgotten."

Toby's heart ached at the sadness in Whistle's voice. He couldn't imagine what it must have been like to be left alone, waiting day after day, with no one to talk to, no one to hear your stories. He placed his hand back on the train's side, feeling the warmth of the connection between them.

"Well, you're not alone anymore," Toby said firmly. "I found you, and I'll keep coming back. You can tell me all your stories, Whistle. I'd love to hear them."

The train seemed to brighten, its windows glinting faintly in the sunlight. "Thank you, Toby. You have no idea how much that means to me," Whistle replied, and Toby thought he heard a hint of happiness in the train's voice.

Toby settled onto the platform beside Whistle, his back against the engine, and looked up at the train. "So, where was your favourite place to go?" he asked, eager to hear more.

Whistle hesitated, as if recalling memories long buried. "Ah, my favourite place... that would be Moonrise Pass. It was high in the mountains, where the tracks wound up and around, and if you looked out the window at the right moment, you'd see the most beautiful view of the valley below. It was especially magical at night, with the stars so close you felt like you could reach out and touch them."

Toby listened, captivated, as Whistle painted a picture with words, describing the places it had been, the people it had met. Each story was filled with wonder, as though Whistle held the memories close to its heart. Toby could almost see it all—the bustling cities, the peaceful countryside, the sweeping mountains and endless skies.

They spent hours like this, with Whistle recounting tales of its journeys and Toby asking questions, eager to know everything about his new friend's past. Whistle told him about a town where every building was painted in bright colors, like a patchwork quilt come to life. Another story was about a festival it had once taken passengers to, where people danced in the streets under a sky filled with lanterns.

After a while, Toby asked, "Did you ever have a best friend? Someone who went with you on all these adventures?"

Whistle paused, and Toby sensed a hint of sadness in the silence that followed. "I did, once," Whistle replied softly. "There was another train, Echo, who used to run on the same tracks. We'd often pass each

TOBY AND THE TALKING TRAIN

other at stations, and we'd whistle to say hello. But that was a long time ago. I don't know what happened to Echo after I was left here."

The thought made Toby's heart ache, and he placed a comforting hand on Whistle's side. "Maybe Echo is still out there somewhere," he said hopefully. "Maybe one day, we could go looking for them."

A soft hum of gratitude filled the air, and Toby felt a warmth spread through him, like he'd done something right, something good. It felt strange to care so much about an old train, but Whistle didn't feel like just a machine. Whistle was alive, with memories, hopes, and dreams of its own.

"Thank you, Toby," Whistle whispered. "You've given me something I thought I'd lost—a friend."

They fell into a comfortable silence, each lost in their own thoughts. Toby found himself thinking about how lucky he was to have stumbled upon Whistle, to have discovered this hidden world of stories and memories. He knew he'd found something special, something that would stay with him for the rest of his life.

As the sun began to dip below the trees, casting golden light across the clearing, Toby realized it was time to head home. He stood up, brushing the dust from his pants, and gave Whistle one last look.

"I'll be back tomorrow," he promised. "And every day after that, if you'll have me."

Whistle's headlights glinted faintly, almost like a smile. "I'll be waiting," the train replied, a warmth in its voice that made Toby's heart swell with happiness.

With a final wave, Toby turned and made his way back along the tracks, his heart brimming with excitement and a deep sense of contentment. He knew he'd found something magical, a friend who could share the stories of places he'd never dreamed of. And as he walked back home, he thought about all the adventures that awaited him, all the stories still untold.

That night, as he lay in bed, Toby felt the strange sense that his life had changed forever. He drifted to sleep with thoughts of Whistle and the sound of the train's soft, gentle voice filling his dreams.

Chapter 3: The Secret Whistle

The days began to pass quickly after Toby's discovery of Whistle. Every chance he got, he'd sneak away to Willow Creek Station, eager to spend time with his new friend. He'd ask Whistle questions about all the far-off places it had seen, listen to tales of magical towns and starlit mountains, and lose himself in the old train's stories. For the first time, Toby felt as if he had a friend who understood him perfectly, someone who shared his love for adventure and mystery.

One chilly autumn afternoon, as Toby sat on the platform swinging his legs, he looked up at Whistle. "I wish I could see you more often," he admitted. "Sometimes, I need a friend to talk to, and I can't always sneak away to the woods."

Whistle let out a thoughtful hum, the kind Toby had come to recognize when the train was deep in thought. The old engine's voice was soft and steady, filled with a wisdom Toby admired. After a few moments, Whistle spoke, a hint of excitement in its tone.

"Well, Toby, perhaps it's time I teach you something special," Whistle said. "Something only my closest friends have ever known."

Toby's eyes widened. He could hardly believe his ears. "Really?" he whispered, leaning forward, his heart pounding with excitement. "What is it?"

Whistle chuckled softly. "It's a whistle," the train explained. "But not just any whistle. This is a secret whistle, one that can call me to you no matter where you are. It's a sound that travels through the air, carried by the wind, reaching me even if you're far away. All you need to do is blow it in just the right way, and I'll come to you."

Toby's eyes sparkled with wonder. A special whistle that could call Whistle whenever he needed him? It sounded like something out of his wildest dreams.

"But… how does it work?" Toby asked, fascinated by the idea.

"I'll teach you," Whistle replied, its headlights flashing slightly as if winking. "It's all in the way you hold your hands and shape your lips. Now, listen closely."

Toby scooted closer, his eyes fixed on Whistle, eager to learn. The train's voice softened as it began to explain the technique.

"First, place your hands together, like this," Whistle instructed, and Toby positioned his hands as best as he could, following the train's guidance. "Then, curl your lips just so, and take a deep breath. You'll need to make a sound that's both soft and high, like the call of a distant bird."

Toby practiced, trying different ways of blowing air between his fingers. At first, all he managed were soft puffs of air and a few squeaks. He laughed, but he was determined to get it right. The idea of having a secret whistle he could use to summon Whistle whenever he needed was too wonderful to give up on.

For nearly an hour, Toby kept trying. Each time he got close, Whistle would offer gentle encouragement. The train's calm voice guided him, offering advice on how to adjust his hands and his breath.

Finally, just as the sun dipped lower in the sky, casting a warm glow over the clearing, Toby tried again. He took a deep breath, positioned his hands, and blew as Whistle had taught him. This time, instead of a soft puff or squeak, a clear, high-pitched whistle echoed through the air.

The sound was beautiful, almost magical. It had a lilting quality, like the song of a far-off bird, carrying through the trees and dancing on the wind. Toby felt a thrill of excitement as the note faded into the forest, knowing he'd finally gotten it right.

"Yes! That's it, Toby!" Whistle exclaimed, its voice filled with pride. "You did it! That's the secret whistle. Now, whenever you're in need, just blow that whistle, and I'll hear it. No matter where I am, I'll find my way to you."

Toby grinned, feeling a rush of pride and joy. He had learned something magical, something that connected him to Whistle in a way that was special, a secret that belonged only to the two of them.

"Thank you, Whistle," he said, his voice filled with gratitude. "I've never had a friend like you."

The train let out a soft hum, a sound Toby had come to recognize as a smile. "And I've never had a friend quite like you, Toby. You've given me something I thought I'd lost—a reason to keep going, to share my stories. That's a gift not every train is lucky enough to receive."

They sat in comfortable silence for a while, watching the sunlight filter through the trees, painting the world in shades of gold and amber. Toby felt a warmth settle over him, a feeling of deep contentment that made him feel lighter than he had in a long time.

As the light began to fade, Toby knew he'd have to head home soon. He stood up, brushing off his hands, and gave Whistle a final, grateful smile.

"Don't worry, I'll be back soon," he promised. "And now, I know how to call you whenever I need you."

Whistle's headlights flickered softly, almost like a nod. "I'll always be listening, Toby. Just use the whistle, and I'll be there."

With a last, lingering look at his friend, Toby turned and began the familiar walk back along the tracks. The sky was painted with hues of pink and orange, and a light breeze rustled through the trees, carrying with it the distant echoes of his secret whistle.

That night, as he lay in bed, Toby thought about Whistle and the magic of their friendship. He imagined all the times he'd use the whistle—maybe when he felt lonely, or when he wanted to share an exciting moment, or when he simply wanted to hear Whistle's calming voice. It was like having a friend who was always just a call away, someone he could trust, no matter what.

In his dreams, he found himself standing in the forest, the whistle's clear, high note ringing out into the night. And as the sound faded,

Whistle would appear, its headlights glowing softly, ready to take him on another adventure.

With a smile on his face, Toby drifted into sleep, feeling the warmth of a friendship unlike any other—a friendship bound by a simple, secret whistle, and a promise that Whistle would always be there when he needed him most.

Chapter 4: A Journey to Yesterday

The day dawned bright and cool, with a sky so clear it felt like an invitation to explore. Toby couldn't wait to get to Willow Creek Station, and he practically skipped through the forest, the sound of his secret whistle still fresh in his mind. He'd practiced it every day since Whistle had taught him, feeling a rush of excitement each time he managed to make the magical sound echo through the trees. But today, as he reached the clearing and saw Whistle waiting at the platform, he sensed that something special was about to happen.

"Good morning, Whistle!" he called, giving the train an enthusiastic wave as he approached.

"Good morning, Toby," Whistle replied, his voice warm and welcoming. "I've been looking forward to seeing you."

Toby grinned, settling himself comfortably beside the old engine. "I was thinking, maybe today you could tell me more stories about the places you've been. I want to hear all about the people you used to meet."

Whistle let out a thoughtful hum. "Oh, I have plenty of stories for you, Toby. But I was thinking... how would you like to see one of those stories for yourself?"

Toby's eyes widened in surprise. "See it? You mean, like actually go somewhere?"

"Yes," Whistle said with a chuckle. "Some journeys are more than just trips along tracks. I have a special kind of journey in mind—one that's a bit different from any you've taken before."

Toby's heart thumped with excitement. He'd always loved Whistle's stories, but the idea of actually traveling to one of those times, of being part of Whistle's memories, was beyond anything he'd imagined.

"So... where would we go?" he asked, his voice filled with wonder.

Whistle hesitated for a moment before answering, his voice soft with a kind of wistful warmth. "I thought I'd take you to meet someone special from your family's past. Someone I knew quite well—a young boy named Thomas. But you might know him better as... your grandfather."

Toby's mouth dropped open. "My grandpa? You knew him when he was little?"

Whistle let out a soft hum of agreement. "Yes, I did. He was about your age when he used to come here to Willow Creek Station, always eager for an adventure. In fact, he was a lot like you, Toby."

Toby could hardly believe it. His grandfather had passed away when Toby was very young, but his parents had often told him stories about the adventures his grandpa had had as a boy. He felt a mixture of excitement and nervousness at the thought of meeting his grandfather in the past, to see him as a boy, to get a glimpse of his family's history firsthand.

"Are you ready, Toby?" Whistle asked, his voice calm and steady.

Toby nodded, bracing himself as he climbed up onto the platform and settled into his usual spot near the engine. He wasn't sure exactly how Whistle would make it happen, but he trusted his friend completely.

"Hold on tight," Whistle said, a note of excitement in his voice. "This may feel a little... different."

Before Toby could ask what he meant, a strange, warm light surrounded him, and the air around them shimmered. The trees and platform faded from view, and for a moment, everything was silent and still. Then, gradually, new sounds began to fill the air—the clatter of footsteps, the soft hum of voices, the distant chugging of trains.

When the light faded, Toby opened his eyes, and his breath caught in his throat. He was still at Willow Creek Station, but it looked entirely different. The building was freshly painted, its bricks vibrant, and the wooden sign overhead gleamed in the sunlight. The platform was bustling with people, men in suits, women in long dresses, and children laughing and running.

Whistle stood beside him, looking newer and shinier than Toby had ever seen him. His green paint glistened, and his windows sparkled, free of dust.

"Are we... did we really go back in time?" Toby whispered, staring in awe at the bustling station.

"Yes, Toby," Whistle replied. "We're in the year 1950, the same year I first met your grandfather."

Toby scanned the platform, his heart racing with excitement. He wondered where his grandpa could be, what he might look like as a young boy. And then, as if drawn by some invisible force, he spotted a young boy standing at the edge of the platform, looking at Whistle with wide, eager eyes.

The boy had tousled brown hair, a mischievous smile, and a curiosity in his gaze that reminded Toby so much of himself. He was holding a small notebook in his hands, scribbling furiously as he looked over the train, jotting down notes and glancing up every few seconds, as though he didn't want to miss a single detail.

Toby's heart skipped a beat. "Is that... is that him?"

Whistle let out a soft hum. "Yes, that's your grandfather, Thomas, when he was just a boy."

Filled with a mixture of excitement and nerves, Toby stepped closer, hoping to get a better look. He watched as young Thomas approached Whistle, placing a small hand on the train's side with a look of awe.

"Hello there, Whistle," young Thomas murmured. "I've never seen a train like you before."

Toby's heart swelled as he listened to his grandfather's voice, younger and filled with wonder. Thomas was looking at Whistle in the same way Toby had, with a spark of friendship that only special people seemed to feel.

Toby stayed close, watching as his grandfather continued to examine the train, asking questions and writing down notes in his little book. He asked about the places Whistle had travelled, the mountains and valleys, the rivers and forests. Whistle answered each question patiently, sharing stories that Toby had already come to know, stories that had connected him to his new friend.

Then, young Thomas paused, looking up at Whistle thoughtfully. "One day, I want to have adventures just like you, Whistle. I want to see the world, meet all kinds of people, and hear their stories."

The words made Toby smile. His grandfather had been just like him, dreaming of far-off places and thrilling journeys. And now, Toby felt like he was part of something much bigger, a family tradition of curiosity and wonder that had started long before him.

As Toby watched, his grandfather's attention turned, and he looked over at him with a curious smile. "Hi," young Thomas said, his voice friendly. "Are you waiting for the train, too?"

Toby hesitated, feeling a flutter of nerves, but he managed a smile. "Yes," he replied softly. "I heard this train is... very special."

Thomas grinned, his eyes lighting up. "It really is! Whistle has been to so many places. One day, I want to go on adventures with him, to places nobody else has ever been." He paused, then added shyly, "Do you like adventures, too?"

Toby nodded, feeling a warmth in his chest. "Yes. I think... I think it runs in my family."

They spent a few more minutes talking, Toby and the young Thomas sharing stories of their imagined adventures. Toby felt an overwhelming sense of pride and joy, seeing the young, adventurous boy his grandfather had been, and he couldn't wait to carry that spirit forward.

Finally, Whistle's voice broke through the moment, gentle but firm. "It's time, Toby."

TOBY AND THE TALKING TRAIN 19

Reluctantly, Toby nodded. He turned to his grandfather, feeling a little emotional. "It was nice to meet you, Thomas," he said, his voice soft. "I hope you have all the adventures you dream of."

Young Thomas smiled, his eyes bright. "Thank you! Maybe one day, we'll see each other again."

Toby stepped back, feeling the warmth of the past as it faded around him. The platform, the sounds, young Thomas—they all shimmered and faded, until Toby found himself back in the quiet clearing at Willow Creek Station. He took a deep breath, feeling the weight of what he'd just experienced settle over him.

Whistle let out a comforting hum. "Did you enjoy the journey, Toby?"

"Yes," Toby whispered, his voice filled with awe. "Thank you, Whistle. I didn't know... I didn't know my grandpa was so much like me."

Whistle's voice was soft and filled with warmth. "The spirit of adventure runs strong in your family, Toby. Your grandfather dreamed of seeing the world, and now you carry on that dream."

Toby smiled, feeling connected to his family's past in a way he never had before. He placed his hand on Whistle's side, filled with gratitude. "Thank you, Whistle. That was the best adventure yet."

As he walked home, Toby knew that he'd carry the memory of this journey forever, a reminder of his grandfather's dreams—and his own. And he knew that, as long as Whistle was by his side, he'd never be alone on the journey.

Chapter 5: The Mysterious Conductor

The morning after his journey into the past, Toby couldn't stop thinking about what he'd experienced. Meeting his grandfather as a young boy had left him with a deep sense of wonder, and he was bursting with questions. But even more than that, he felt the need to return to Whistle. He had a sense that there was so much more to discover, mysteries about Whistle and Willow Creek Station that he had only just begun to unravel.

As he hurried through the forest, sunlight filtering through the trees and casting patterns on the ground, Toby felt a shiver of anticipation. He could feel something in the air, a kind of hum that made his heart beat faster. When he reached the clearing, he found Whistle waiting for him, looking as timeless and patient as ever.

"Good morning, Whistle!" Toby called out as he approached.

"Good morning, Toby," Whistle replied warmly. "I can see you've got questions swirling around in that curious mind of yours."

Toby laughed, nodding. "I do! There's so much I want to know about you, about the station, and... everything, really!"

Whistle chuckled, his voice deep and warm. "Well, Toby, I might have just the answer for you today. There's someone you should meet. Someone who knows more about the hidden world of magical trains than anyone else."

Toby's eyes widened in excitement. "Someone else knows about you? Who is it?"

At that moment, a soft rustling came from the trees at the edge of the clearing. Toby turned, his heart pounding, and watched as a tall, slender figure emerged from the forest. The figure was dressed in a deep blue conductor's uniform, complete with a cap and a polished silver whistle that hung around her neck. Her eyes sparkled with a strange, knowing light, and she moved with a graceful, almost ethereal presence.

"Hello, Toby," she said, her voice as soft as a breeze but filled with a calm authority. "I've been looking forward to meeting you."

Toby felt an instant connection to her, as though she were someone he'd always known, even though he'd never seen her before. "Are you... are you a conductor?" he asked, his voice barely a whisper.

The woman smiled, her eyes twinkling. "Yes, I am. My name is Conductor Clara. I'm the caretaker of Willow Creek Station and the protector of all magical trains, including Whistle here." She gave Whistle an affectionate pat, and the train let out a low hum of contentment.

Toby stared in awe, his mind buzzing with questions. "You mean... there are more magical trains like Whistle?"

Conductor Clara nodded. "Oh, yes. Whistle is one of many trains with a voice, a spirit, and a story all their own. Some are hidden in forests like this one, others lie deep within mountains, and some even glide along tracks that stretch across enchanted deserts."

Toby's eyes widened, his imagination running wild with images of magical trains racing through mystical landscapes. "Why haven't I ever heard about them before? Why do they stay hidden?"

Clara's expression grew serious, and she knelt down to look Toby in the eye. "The world of magical trains is a world of secrets, Toby. These trains have powers and knowledge that must be protected. Long ago, they were seen and celebrated by people who understood them, but as time went on, fewer people could hear their voices. So the trains became hidden, waiting for those with open hearts and curious minds to find them."

Toby felt a thrill run through him. He was one of the few people who could hear Whistle, one of the few who was trusted to know about this hidden world. "Does that mean... I'm one of those people?"

Clara smiled. "Yes, Toby. You have a gift. Not everyone can hear Whistle speak, and even fewer would be able to connect with him as you have. You're part of a special group known as the Listeners."

"The Listeners?" Toby repeated, his heart racing.

Clara nodded. "Listeners are those who can hear the voices of magical trains, people who can understand and share their stories. It's a rare gift, and it comes with a great responsibility. Whistle chose you because he sensed the kindness and bravery in your heart."

Toby looked at Whistle, feeling a surge of gratitude and pride. He had always felt a deep connection to the train, but now he understood that it was something rare, something precious.

Clara placed a gentle hand on Toby's shoulder. "But remember, Toby, the world of magical trains is full of mysteries, some of which even I don't fully understand. There are places that only trains like Whistle can reach, places that hold secrets from ancient times. It's a world where time and space work differently, where the ordinary rules don't always apply."

Toby felt a sense of awe wash over him. He looked up at Clara, his eyes filled with questions. "Do you know everything about Whistle? About where he's been and what he's seen?"

Conductor Clara chuckled softly, a hint of mystery in her gaze. "I know much about Whistle and the journeys he's taken, but even I don't know all his secrets. Each train has memories it holds close, memories it shares only with those it truly trusts. That's why it's important for you to listen, to be patient, and to earn Whistle's trust over time."

Toby nodded, feeling the weight of the responsibility Clara was talking about. He looked at Whistle, realizing that his friendship with the train was something he would cherish and protect with all his heart.

Clara's eyes softened as she looked at the two friends. "I have something for you, Toby," she said, reaching into her coat pocket and pulling out a small, silver whistle. It was intricately carved with swirling patterns that seemed to shimmer in the light.

"This is a Listener's Whistle," Clara explained, holding it out to Toby. "It's different from the whistle Whistle taught you. This one can call upon any magical train in need or connect you to me. If you ever find yourself lost or in danger, just blow this whistle, and help will find its way to you."

Toby took the silver whistle, his hands trembling slightly as he held it. The metal felt warm, almost alive, and he could feel a faint hum of energy pulsing from it. "Thank you, Conductor Clara," he said, his voice filled with gratitude. "I'll take good care of it."

Clara gave him an approving nod. "I know you will, Toby. Remember, being a Listener means respecting the magic of the trains, keeping their secrets, and helping them when they need it. It's a bond of trust, one that I know you'll honour."

With that, she straightened up, a mysterious smile playing on her lips. "I have other stations to tend to, and other trains who need my guidance. But I'll be around when you need me, Toby. Just remember—you're part of a magical world now, and it will look after you as long as you look after it."

Toby watched as Conductor Clara took a few steps back, her figure seeming to blend into the forest shadows. She lifted a hand in farewell, her eyes twinkling with a quiet knowledge, and then, with a soft rustling of leaves, she disappeared into the trees.

He stood in silence for a moment, staring at the spot where she had been, still holding the silver whistle in his hand. He felt a thrill of excitement, but also a sense of responsibility. He was part of something ancient and magical, a world filled with secrets and wonders beyond his imagination.

Toby turned to Whistle, a new resolve in his eyes. "I promise, Whistle. I'll be a good Listener. I'll keep your secrets safe and be the best friend I can be."

Whistle let out a low hum, a sound of gratitude and pride. "Thank you, Toby. I knew from the moment I saw you that you were special."

As the sun began to dip below the trees, casting long shadows across the clearing, Toby knew that his life had changed in a way he was only beginning to understand. He felt a sense of purpose, a feeling of belonging to a magical world that few would ever know.

With the Listener's Whistle tucked carefully into his pocket, Toby said goodbye to Whistle for the day, his heart brimming with excitement and wonder. And as he made his way home, he knew that his adventures with Whistle had only just begun, and that Conductor Clara's world of magical trains was waiting, full of mysteries and magic yet to be discovered.

Chapter 6: The First Magical Lesson

The next time Toby returned to Willow Creek Station, he felt a sense of excitement and curiosity he hadn't felt before. Meeting Conductor Clara had opened his eyes to a new world of magical trains and hidden secrets. He now understood that being a Listener came with responsibilities, and he was eager to learn more about what it meant.

As he approached Whistle, the train greeted him with a warm, familiar hum. Toby placed a hand on the side of the engine, feeling the connection between them grow stronger with each visit.

"Good morning, Whistle!" Toby said brightly. "I've been thinking a lot about everything Conductor Clara told me. I want to be the best Listener I can be."

Whistle chuckled, his deep, soothing voice filled with warmth. "I know you will be, Toby. And today, I'd like to teach you something that every Listener—and every magical train—knows well. It's the first lesson I ever learned: the importance of kindness."

Toby tilted his head, intrigued. "Kindness? You mean like being nice to people?"

Whistle let out a soft hum, a sound that felt like a gentle nod. "Yes, but it's more than just being nice. Kindness is about helping others, even when it's difficult, and looking out for those in need. For magical trains like me, kindness is how we stay connected, how we support each other on the tracks that stretch far beyond this forest."

Toby felt a warm sense of understanding but was eager to know more. "How do trains help each other, though? I mean, you're all... well, trains! Do you talk to each other like we do?"

"Indeed we do," Whistle replied, his voice soft and full of memories. "We communicate in different ways. Sometimes, it's through the vibrations in the tracks; other times, it's through the wind and the echoes of our whistles. And whenever one of us is in trouble, the others will always come to help."

Toby's eyes sparkled with fascination. He imagined a network of magical trains, always listening out for one another, sharing both joy and struggle. "Can you show me? I'd love to see how it works!"

With a low hum of agreement, Whistle began to stir. "Hold on tight, Toby. I'll take you to a place where the trains come together—a place where kindness is needed most."

Toby felt a thrill of excitement as he settled down beside Whistle. A familiar glow of light surrounded them, the trees and platform blurring and fading as they embarked on yet another magical journey. When the light cleared, they found themselves on a high mountain pass, with breathtaking views stretching as far as the eye could see.

The tracks here seemed to glimmer in the sunlight, twisting and winding along steep cliffs and through narrow tunnels. And just ahead, Toby saw a line of trains gathered on the tracks, their engines humming softly as if they were communicating.

Toby stared in awe. He had never seen so many trains in one place, and each one looked different from the last. There was a sleek, silver train with a bright blue stripe, a sturdy, red engine covered in patches of soot, and even a small, colorful train with carriages painted in cheerful patterns.

"Why are they all here?" Toby whispered, captivated by the sight.

Whistle let out a soft sigh. "They're here to help. One of our own, a train named Rusty, got caught on a broken stretch of track up ahead. She's stuck, unable to move forward or back. The others have come to offer their assistance."

Toby watched as the trains began to work together in perfect harmony. One train pulled up behind Rusty, gently nudging her forward, while another train secured ropes and chains, preparing to tow her over the damaged section of track. Meanwhile, a third train let out a powerful whistle, signalling to the others to hold steady as they worked.

It was a beautiful sight—each train helping in its own way, contributing whatever it could to make sure Rusty was safe. Toby felt a swell of admiration for them all.

"This is kindness in action, Toby," Whistle said quietly. "When one of us is in trouble, the others don't hesitate to lend a hand. It's not always easy; sometimes, helping others means risking our own safety. But that's what it means to be connected, to be part of something larger than ourselves."

Toby nodded, his heart full of understanding. "I never knew trains could do so much for each other," he murmured. "It's like they're all... family."

Whistle let out a gentle hum. "Yes, Toby. In many ways, we are a family. And kindness is what keeps us together, even when the tracks are rough or the journey is long."

Toby watched as the trains continued their efforts, each one contributing what it could. And finally, after a few minutes, Rusty was pulled free from the broken track. The gathered trains let out a triumphant whistle, their voices blending together in a symphony of joy.

Rusty, now back on solid ground, let out a soft, grateful whistle in return. "Thank you, everyone," she said, her voice shaky with relief. "I don't know what I would have done without you."

The other trains let out reassuring hums and whistles, and slowly, they began to disperse, returning to their own journeys. Toby felt a warmth spread through him as he watched them go, understanding now the true power of kindness and connection.

Turning to Whistle, Toby said, "Thank you for showing me this. I think I understand now. Kindness isn't just about what you do for yourself—it's about what you do for others, even when it's hard."

Whistle let out a pleased hum. "You've got it, Toby. Being a Listener means hearing more than just our voices. It means understanding the importance of helping, of being there for others whenever they need you."

Toby thought about his family, his friends, and even people he didn't know. He realized that he could bring kindness into his own world, just as the magical trains did.

As they made their way back to Willow Creek Station, Toby thought about all the ways he could help others, about the times he might have ignored someone who needed help, or failed to notice when someone was struggling. He felt a new sense of purpose—a desire to bring the lessons he'd learned from Whistle into his own life.

When they arrived back at the clearing, Toby climbed off the platform and turned to face Whistle, his eyes shining with gratitude.

"Thank you, Whistle," he said softly. "I think kindness is one of the best things anyone can learn. And I promise, I'll try to be kind every day, just like the trains you showed me."

Whistle let out a gentle, approving hum. "That's all any of us can do, Toby. Kindness has a way of making the world feel smaller, of bringing people—and trains—together."

With a smile, Toby gave Whistle a final wave and started his journey back through the forest. His heart felt lighter, and he carried with him a newfound determination to spread kindness wherever he went.

As he walked, he thought of Rusty and the other trains, and he realized that kindness was a form of magic in itself—one that connected everyone, no matter how different they might seem.

Toby knew he was ready to take this lesson with him, to be not just a Listener, but a friend to everyone who needed one, just as the trains had been friends to each other.

And as he walked, he imagined Whistle beside him, guiding him with the gentle hum of wisdom that he'd come to love.

Chapter 7: The Lost Toy Adventure

It was a crisp autumn morning when Toby arrived at Willow Creek Station, his cheeks rosy from the brisk walk through the woods. He found Whistle waiting for him, humming softly in the morning sunlight, as if the train was eager for an adventure.

"Good morning, Whistle!" Toby greeted, settling onto the platform beside his friend.

"Good morning, Toby," Whistle replied warmly. "I hope you're ready for something special today. There's a bit of a mission that needs our help."

Toby's eyes lit up with excitement. Missions with Whistle always meant some kind of adventure, something new to learn. "What kind of mission?"

Whistle let out a gentle hum. "Last night, I received a message from one of my old friends, Patches the cargo train. A little boy named Oliver from a nearby town lost his favourite toy during a trip, and Patches spotted it lying on the tracks. But Oliver's town is far, and Patches isn't able to leave his route today. So, I thought we could help retrieve it and bring it back to him."

Toby's heart swelled at the thought of helping someone in need, especially a child like himself. He imagined how devastated he would feel if he lost one of his favourite toys. "Let's do it!" he said eagerly. "What kind of toy is it?"

"It's a small wooden train, carved and painted by hand," Whistle explained. "It has a red engine and three little carriages. Oliver's grandfather made it for him, and he takes it with him wherever he goes. Losing it must have been heartbreaking for him."

Toby nodded, feeling a sense of responsibility settle over him. He knew that bringing back Oliver's toy would mean a lot to the little boy. And he felt a new sense of purpose—to make sure it reached him safely.

"Hold on, Toby," Whistle said with a chuckle. "We have a bit of ground to cover."

With that, Toby took his usual seat beside Whistle, and the familiar warmth and light of their magical journeys surrounded them. The trees and station blurred, and when the light cleared, they found themselves on a long stretch of track, bordered by green fields and tall trees swaying in the wind.

"Patches mentioned he saw the toy near the Maple Junction bridge," Whistle said, his voice thoughtful. "Keep an eye out; it's small, but it should be around here somewhere."

Toby peered along the tracks as Whistle slowed down, watching carefully for any sign of the toy train. His heart pounded with a mixture of excitement and focus. He wanted to be the one to spot it, to make sure they didn't miss it.

After a few minutes, Toby's keen eyes caught a flash of red among the stones along the side of the tracks. "There! I see it!" he cried, pointing.

Whistle slowed to a gentle stop, and Toby jumped down onto the gravel, approaching the small wooden train carefully. It lay there, slightly dusty but still intact, its red paint gleaming in the sunlight.

Toby picked it up, feeling the smooth wood under his fingers. It was a beautiful toy, lovingly crafted with little details carved into each carriage. He could tell it had been cherished and well-cared-for, with a few tiny scratches and dents that gave it character.

"This must mean so much to Oliver," Toby murmured, feeling the weight of the responsibility he held in his hands. "We have to get it back to him safely."

As he climbed back up to Whistle, he held the wooden train carefully in his lap, almost as if it were made of glass. He wanted to make sure it reached Oliver in the same condition he'd found it.

"Good eye, Toby," Whistle said approvingly. "Now, we just need to make our way to Oliver's town."

Toby settled into his seat, feeling a mixture of pride and responsibility. He was determined to keep the toy safe and make sure it reached Oliver just as he'd left it.

As they travelled, Toby thought about what it would mean to lose something as precious as this toy. He thought of his favourite belongings, the things that had been with him through countless adventures and quiet moments. He realized how much they meant to him, not because they were just objects, but because they held memories and feelings.

"Toys aren't just toys, are they, Whistle?" Toby said quietly. "They're... they're like friends, in a way."

Whistle let out a gentle hum of agreement. "That's true, Toby. The things we love often carry pieces of our lives with them. And when we lose them, it can feel like we've lost a part of ourselves."

Toby nodded, looking down at the little wooden train. "That's why it's so important to take care of the things we love. And to help others take care of the things they love, too."

They travelled along the tracks until the rooftops of a small town came into view. The houses were quaint, with colorful gardens and picket fences, and the town had a cozy feel to it. Whistle let out a soft whistle as they approached the town's station, alerting the townspeople to their arrival.

Toby noticed a young boy standing with his mother on the platform, his shoulders slumped and his face drawn in sadness. The boy clutched his mother's hand, but his gaze was distant, as though he were lost in thought.

"That must be Oliver," Toby whispered to Whistle, his heart aching at the sight of the boy's sorrow.

"Go on, Toby," Whistle encouraged. "You're the one who should give him back his lost friend."

Taking a deep breath, Toby climbed down from the platform, holding the little wooden train in his hands. He walked over to Oliver, who looked up as Toby approached, his eyes widening when he saw the toy.

"Is this... is this yours?" Toby asked, smiling gently as he held out the train.

Oliver gasped, his face lighting up with a mixture of shock and joy. He reached out, his hands trembling, and took the wooden train, holding it as if it were the most precious thing in the world.

"Yes! It's mine! Thank you, thank you so much!" Oliver exclaimed, clutching the toy to his chest. His eyes filled with happy tears, and he looked up at Toby with a smile that was brighter than the morning sun. "I thought it was lost forever!"

Toby felt a surge of happiness at the sight of Oliver's joy. It was a feeling unlike any other, a warmth that spread through his heart, knowing he had made a difference in someone's life. "I'm glad we could find it for you," Toby said, smiling back. "I know how much it means to you."

Oliver's mother placed a gentle hand on Toby's shoulder. "Thank you so much, young man," she said warmly. "You've given him something he thought he'd never see again."

Toby nodded, feeling a sense of pride in what he'd done. He glanced back at Whistle, who watched from the platform, his headlights glowing softly as though smiling.

After saying goodbye to Oliver and his mother, Toby climbed back up onto the platform, feeling a deep sense of accomplishment. As they began their journey back to Willow Creek Station, he reflected on what he'd learned.

"Helping Oliver made me realize something, Whistle," he said thoughtfully. "Responsibility isn't just about taking care of our own things. It's about helping others, too. Making sure that the things they care about are safe."

Whistle let out a soft hum, a sound that seemed to hold both pride and encouragement. "Well said, Toby. Responsibility is about more than just ourselves—it's about the world around us. And you showed true responsibility today by caring for something precious to someone else."

As they returned to the familiar forest, Toby felt a new sense of purpose within him. He understood that being a Listener, and being Whistle's friend, came with responsibilities that went beyond himself. It was about being someone others could rely on, someone who cared not just for his own world but for others' as well.

With the day's adventure behind him, Toby walked back home, his heart light and his mind full of thoughts. He felt a deeper understanding of what it meant to be responsible, to take care of the things—and people—that mattered. He knew that this lesson, like so many others he'd learned with Whistle, would stay with him for a long time.

And as he looked forward to the next adventure, he couldn't wait to discover what other lessons awaited him in the magical world of Willow Creek Station.

Chapter 8: Whistle's Sad Story

Toby couldn't wait to get to Willow Creek Station. The days he spent with Whistle always left him feeling lighter, wiser, and more connected to the magical world that most people never saw. But as he approached the clearing this morning, he noticed something different about his friend. Whistle was unusually quiet, his headlights dim, and a sombre air seemed to hang around him.

"Good morning, Whistle," Toby said softly as he approached, sensing that something was troubling the train.

"Good morning, Toby," Whistle replied, his voice gentle but with an unmistakable heaviness.

Toby climbed up onto the platform and placed a comforting hand on the side of the train. "Are you alright, Whistle? You seem... sad today."

Whistle let out a low hum, one that sounded almost like a sigh. "There are some days, Toby, when I think back on my past and feel the weight of my memories. Today is one of those days."

Toby's curiosity and concern deepened. In all their time together, he'd never heard Whistle sound so wistful, so filled with sorrow. He wanted to help, to understand what was troubling his friend.

"Whistle, you can tell me anything," Toby said gently. "I'm here for you."

There was a long pause as Whistle seemed to gather his thoughts. Finally, the train spoke, his voice softer than usual, as though sharing a secret long buried.

"A long time ago, I wasn't just a train waiting here in the woods," Whistle began. "I was part of a bustling railway, one that connected towns and cities, places brimming with people and life. My days were filled with the sounds of laughter, the thrill of travellers boarding for their journeys, and the joy of seeing new places."

Toby nodded, picturing the lively scenes Whistle was describing. He could almost see it in his mind—Whistle rolling through towns, his green and red paint gleaming, his whistle cutting through the air with a happy, welcoming sound.

"But one day," Whistle continued, his voice tinged with sadness, "the world began to change. Newer, faster trains came along—trains that could go farther and carry more people. They didn't need trains like me anymore. And so, I was sent to Willow Creek Station, my tracks no longer part of any map, my routes forgotten. I was abandoned."

The words hung in the air, filling Toby's heart with a deep ache. He couldn't imagine what it must have felt like for Whistle to go from a life of adventure and purpose to being left alone, hidden in the forest, with only memories for company.

"Whistle... that must have been so hard for you," Toby said softly, his hand resting on the side of the train as if to comfort him.

Whistle let out a low hum, one that vibrated with a quiet sorrow. "For a long time, it was. I'd spent years connecting people, carrying them to places they dreamed of visiting. Suddenly, I was no longer needed, no longer part of anyone's journey. I sat here, day after day, waiting and hoping that someone might come. But as the seasons passed, I began to lose hope."

Toby felt tears prick his eyes. He couldn't bear the thought of Whistle sitting alone for so long, waiting in silence, surrounded by nothing but the whispering trees and the rustling leaves. "I'm so sorry, Whistle. You deserved better."

Whistle gave a gentle hum, as if accepting Toby's compassion. "Thank you, Toby. But then, something changed. I started to notice the beauty around me—the forest, the way the sunlight would filter through the leaves, the sound of birds singing. I realized that even in this quiet place, there was still a kind of magic. I just had to listen for it."

Toby nodded, understanding. Whistle had found a way to find peace, even in his solitude. But he also knew that it must have been incredibly lonely.

"And then... you came along," Whistle said softly, his voice filled with warmth and gratitude. "When I first saw you, I couldn't believe it. After so many years, someone had finally found me. Someone who could hear my voice, who wanted to know my stories. You brought life back to this station, Toby. You gave me hope again."

Toby's heart swelled with emotion. He felt honoured to have brought Whistle even a fraction of the joy the train had brought him. He reached out, placing both hands on Whistle's side as if to make his promise all the more real.

"I'll never leave you, Whistle," he said firmly. "You're my friend, and I promise I'll always be here for you."

There was a long, warm silence as Toby's words settled into the stillness of the forest. Finally, Whistle let out a soft hum, one filled with a mixture of relief and happiness.

"Thank you, Toby," Whistle whispered. "You have no idea what that means to me."

Toby took a deep breath, feeling a surge of responsibility and friendship. He wanted to be the best friend he could to Whistle, to make up for all the years his friend had spent alone. But more than that, he wanted Whistle to know that he was no longer forgotten, that he was valued and loved.

"Is there anything I can do to help you feel better, Whistle?" Toby asked gently, wanting to offer more than just words.

Whistle was quiet for a moment before responding. "You already have, Toby. You've given me something more valuable than you know—a friend who cares, who listens, who shares his own stories and dreams. That's all I need."

Toby smiled, feeling a sense of peace settle over him. He knew that their friendship went both ways, that he had as much to learn from

Whistle as Whistle had to share. It was a bond that felt timeless, as if it had always been there, waiting for him to discover.

They sat in companionable silence, watching the sun filter through the trees, casting gentle patterns of light and shadow across the station. For the first time, Toby saw Willow Creek Station through Whistle's eyes—as a place filled with memories, with traces of the people and adventures that had passed through it over the years.

And though the world had changed, leaving Whistle behind, Toby felt a quiet determination to make sure his friend was never forgotten again. He would carry Whistle's stories with him, sharing them with anyone who would listen, so that Whistle's legacy would live on.

As the sun began to dip lower in the sky, Toby turned to his friend, a new idea forming in his mind. "You know, Whistle, we could make some new memories. We don't have to just think about the past—we can create new adventures, right here, together."

Whistle let out a soft, hopeful hum. "I would like that very much, Toby."

With a promise to return soon, Toby said goodbye and started his walk back through the forest. As he walked, he thought about Whistle's story, about the lessons of resilience and hope his friend had shown him. He understood now that even the hardest times could be softened by friendship, by the kindness of someone who cared.

And he knew, deep in his heart, that he would keep coming back to Willow Creek Station, not just because of the magic, but because of the unbreakable bond he had with Whistle. Together, they would keep the spirit of adventure alive, one story at a time.

Toby felt a sense of gratitude and purpose as he made his way home. He knew that he would always carry Whistle's story with him, a reminder that even in the quietest corners of the world, friendship could be found and memories could be made.

Chapter 9: Toby's Secret World

Over the next few days, Toby found himself more enchanted with Whistle than ever. Every moment he spent at Willow Creek Station felt like a new adventure, each one filled with stories, lessons, and the quiet, reassuring presence of his friend. But there was one thing that weighed on Toby's mind: Whistle was his secret, and secrets were harder to keep than he'd imagined.

At first, the secret had felt magical, a special bond between him and Whistle, something wonderful he had all to himself. But now, every time he returned from the forest, his parents and friends would ask where he'd been, what he'd been doing. Toby's answers always felt rushed and vague. He didn't want to lie, but he couldn't tell them about Whistle, either. This was something too special, too fragile, and he knew that he needed to protect it.

One evening, as he sat at the dinner table, his mother looked at him curiously. "You've been spending a lot of time in the woods lately, Toby," she said, her voice gentle but questioning. "What have you been up to?"

Toby's heart pounded, and he tried to think of a response. "Oh, just... exploring," he mumbled, poking at his food.

His father raised an eyebrow, smiling. "Exploring, huh? You're not getting into any trouble, are you?"

Toby quickly shook his head. "No! I'm just... looking around. The forest is really cool."

His mother and father exchanged a glance, but they didn't press him further. Still, Toby could feel the weight of their curiosity, and he wondered if he'd be able to keep Whistle a secret much longer. He knew they'd love to hear about his adventures, but he wasn't ready to share Whistle with anyone else. It felt as though saying it out loud would break the magic somehow.

At school, his friends noticed the change in him, too. His best friend, Leo, asked him about it during recess one day.

"Hey, Toby, you've been really quiet lately. And you're always running off after school. Are you okay?" Leo's face was filled with genuine concern, and Toby felt a pang of guilt.

"I'm fine," Toby said, trying to sound casual. "I've just... been busy with some stuff."

Leo tilted his head, looking confused. "What kind of stuff? We used to go exploring together, remember? It's no fun without you."

Toby forced a smile, feeling torn. He wanted to tell Leo about Whistle, to share the wonder of the hidden station and the magic of his friend, but he wasn't sure if he could trust anyone else with something so precious.

"It's just... it's hard to explain," he muttered, hoping Leo would let it go.

But Leo only frowned, looking hurt. "Alright, fine. I guess if you don't want to tell me, you don't have to," he said, turning away.

The guilt gnawed at Toby for the rest of the day. He missed spending time with Leo, and he hated the idea of his friend feeling left out. But he couldn't risk losing Whistle by sharing his secret. He had promised Whistle that he'd protect their friendship, and he didn't want to break that promise.

Later that day, as Toby made his way to Willow Creek Station, his thoughts weighed heavily on him. When he arrived, he found Whistle waiting, as always, a comforting presence in the quiet clearing.

"Hello, Toby," Whistle greeted, his voice calm and steady. "You seem troubled."

Toby sighed, settling down on the platform. "It's just... it's hard keeping you a secret. My parents and friends keep asking where I've been, and I don't know what to tell them. I feel like I'm lying to everyone."

Whistle let out a thoughtful hum. "I understand, Toby. Secrets can be heavy, especially when they're about something as special as our friendship."

Toby looked down, fiddling with a stray pebble on the platform. "I don't want to keep things from my family and friends. But I'm also scared that if I tell them about you, it'll ruin everything. What if they don't understand? What if... they don't believe me?"

Whistle was quiet for a moment, his headlights flickering softly as though deep in thought. "Toby, trust is a powerful thing. And sometimes, trust means knowing who to share things with—and who to keep things from, to protect what matters most."

Toby nodded, slowly understanding. "So... it's okay to have a secret if it's to protect someone?"

"Yes," Whistle replied gently. "Sometimes, secrets are a way of honouring something precious. And other times, sharing a secret with someone you truly trust can make that bond even stronger. The question is: do you feel ready to share, or do you feel it's best kept between us?"

Toby thought carefully about Whistle's words. He knew that his family and friends cared about him, and he felt safe with them. But Whistle's friendship was so different, so delicate. He didn't want anyone to misunderstand or interfere with it.

"I think... I think I'm not ready to share it yet," Toby admitted, feeling a strange relief as he said it out loud. "Maybe someday, but for now, I want this to be our secret."

Whistle let out a warm, approving hum. "Then that's exactly what it will be, Toby. You are honouring our friendship by protecting it. But remember, when you are ready, those who truly care about you will listen and understand."

Toby nodded, feeling a newfound sense of peace. He knew that his secret wasn't a lie—it was a promise, a trust he was choosing to keep.

And when the time was right, he would know who he could share it with.

The days that followed felt lighter somehow. Toby found ways to answer his parents' questions honestly without giving too much away. He told them about the things he was learning in the forest, about the quiet and the beauty of nature, and they seemed satisfied. And when he saw Leo, he made an effort to spend time with him, even if he couldn't tell him everything.

But he also realized that keeping Whistle a secret made their friendship even more special. Each day he returned to the station, he felt a thrill knowing that this was a world only he and Whistle shared, a magical place that belonged to them alone.

One afternoon, as he sat beside Whistle on the platform, he felt a surge of gratitude.

"Thank you, Whistle," Toby said softly. "For trusting me, and for helping me understand what it means to protect something important."

Whistle let out a gentle, contented hum. "Thank you, Toby, for being a friend who values trust and understands the importance of loyalty. Those are rare qualities, and they mean more than you know."

Toby smiled, feeling a warmth fill his chest. He knew that his friendship with Whistle was something unique, something worth cherishing. And as he watched the sun dip lower in the sky, casting golden light across the clearing, he felt a quiet pride in the bond they shared.

He had learned that trust wasn't just about sharing everything—it was about knowing when to hold something close, to protect it with everything he had. And as long as he had Whistle by his side, he knew he'd always have a friend he could trust, someone who would be there for him, no matter what.

With a final, grateful pat on Whistle's side, Toby stood up, ready to head home. His secret world remained intact, a place of wonder and friendship that he carried in his heart. And as he walked back through the forest, he felt stronger and wiser, knowing he had learned one of the most important lessons of all—the true value of trust.

Chapter 10: The Lightning Storm Ride

The day had started like any other, with Toby eagerly heading to Willow Creek Station to see Whistle. The sky was bright blue, dotted with a few fluffy clouds, and the air was warm and inviting. But as Toby entered the clearing, he noticed a change. Dark clouds were gathering on the horizon, and a chill wind began to stir the leaves, making the once peaceful woods feel tense and watchful.

"Looks like a storm might be coming," Toby said, glancing up at the sky as he approached Whistle.

Whistle let out a low hum, his headlights flickering slightly. "Yes, Toby. And if I remember anything about these parts, it's that storms here can be powerful and sudden. Are you feeling up for a ride today?"

Toby's heart raced with excitement, mixed with a tinge of nervousness. He'd never been out with Whistle in a storm, but the idea of facing something so powerful, so unpredictable, made him feel a surge of bravery.

"Yes," Toby said, trying to sound confident. "I trust you, Whistle. Let's go!"

As he climbed aboard and settled into his usual spot, a rumble of thunder echoed in the distance, like the growl of some far-off creature. The dark clouds crept closer, thickening as the wind began to pick up, swirling through the trees and sending leaves scattering.

With a low whistle, Whistle started down the tracks, picking up speed as they headed deeper into the woods. The storm gathered quickly, darkening the sky, until it felt like twilight had fallen over them, even though it was midday. The air crackled with energy, and Toby could feel the tension growing, like the whole world was holding its breath.

Then, with a blinding flash, a bolt of lightning split the sky, followed by a deafening clap of thunder that seemed to shake the ground beneath them. Toby felt a jolt of fear, gripping the edge of the platform as the storm roared to life around them.

"Don't be afraid, Toby," Whistle said, his voice calm and steady. "Storms may be powerful, but remember—they're just a part of nature. We'll face this together."

Toby took a deep breath, steadying himself. Whistle's reassurance calmed his nerves, and he felt a flicker of bravery grow inside him. He trusted Whistle, and he knew that his friend would keep him safe, no matter what.

As they continued along the tracks, the rain began to fall in heavy sheets, pounding against Whistle's metal frame and drenching the world around them. The wind howled through the trees, bending branches and scattering leaves across the tracks. Thunder rumbled constantly, sometimes close, sometimes far, each clap making Toby jump despite himself.

With every flash of lightning, the forest around them was illuminated in sharp, eerie detail—the twisted branches, the slick, shining tracks, the shadows cast by the trees. The storm was wild, fierce, and unpredictable, and Toby could feel its power vibrating in the air. But with Whistle's steady hum beneath him, he felt a growing determination to face it head-on.

The rain grew heavier, and the tracks ahead became slick and difficult to see. But Whistle slowed down, carefully navigating each curve and dip, his headlights cutting through the downpour.

"Bravery isn't about never feeling afraid, Toby," Whistle said, his voice steady and wise. "It's about moving forward, even when fear tries to hold you back."

Toby nodded, feeling the words sink into his heart. He knew Whistle was right. The fear he felt was real, but so was the strength that came from pushing through it, from trusting Whistle and his own courage.

TOBY AND THE TALKING TRAIN

As they travelled deeper into the storm, Toby felt himself grow bolder, sitting up straighter and keeping his eyes fixed on the tracks ahead. He no longer flinched at every crash of thunder or flash of lightning. Instead, he focused on the steady rhythm of Whistle's wheels on the tracks, the powerful hum of the engine, and the way his friend moved confidently through the storm, undeterred.

Suddenly, a huge flash of lightning struck a tree just ahead, splitting it down the middle with a loud crack. The tree toppled over, blocking the tracks in front of them.

"Hang on, Toby!" Whistle called out, and Toby braced himself as Whistle slowed to a stop just in time, halting mere feet from the fallen tree.

The storm raged around them, the rain pelting down and the wind whipping through the clearing. Toby stared at the massive tree trunk lying across the tracks, feeling a fresh surge of fear. They were stuck, and the storm showed no signs of letting up.

"What do we do now, Whistle?" Toby asked, his voice shaky.

Whistle let out a reassuring hum. "We'll need to be brave, Toby. Sometimes, bravery means waiting patiently until it's safe to move forward. This storm will pass, and when it does, we'll find a way to continue."

Toby took a deep breath, letting Whistle's words calm him. He realized that bravery wasn't just about action; sometimes, it meant being patient, staying steady, and trusting that things would get better.

They sat together, waiting as the storm raged on around them. Thunder crashed, and lightning danced across the sky, but Toby held on, feeling the strength of Whistle beside him. He realized that just being there, facing the storm together, was an act of courage in itself.

After what felt like a long time, the rain began to ease, softening to a steady drizzle, and the thunder grew distant, rumbling softly as it moved away. The sky lightened, and the dark clouds began to part, revealing patches of blue.

Toby let out a breath he hadn't realized he'd been holding. He felt a deep sense of relief and pride—they had faced the storm together, and they had made it through.

Once the rain stopped completely, Whistle let out a cheerful whistle. "See, Toby? Storms may be fierce, but they always pass. And now, we have a story to tell about how we braved the lightning and thunder."

Toby smiled, feeling a new sense of strength within him. He looked at the fallen tree blocking the tracks and thought for a moment.

"Do you think we could find another way around?" he asked, feeling more determined than ever to keep moving forward.

Whistle chuckled. "There's always another way, Toby. Sometimes, you just have to look for it."

Together, they backed up and took a different route, moving slowly but surely along a winding set of tracks that led them around the fallen tree. As they moved forward, Toby felt a sense of accomplishment, knowing that he and Whistle had faced the storm and come out stronger on the other side.

When they finally returned to Willow Creek Station, the sun was shining brightly, casting a warm glow over the clearing. The storm had passed, leaving the world refreshed and renewed.

Toby climbed down from Whistle, feeling both tired and exhilarated. He looked up at his friend, his heart full of gratitude. "Thank you, Whistle. I don't think I could have faced that storm without you."

Whistle let out a soft, contented hum. "You had the bravery inside you all along, Toby. I was just here to remind you of it."

As Toby made his way back through the forest, he felt stronger, wiser, and more courageous than ever. He knew that storms, whether real or metaphorical, would come and go. But with Whistle's lessons in his heart, he was ready to face them all, one brave step at a time.

Chapter 11: The Friendly Fox

The forest was alive with the sights and sounds of early autumn, golden leaves fluttering to the ground and a gentle breeze weaving through the trees. Toby walked briskly down the familiar path toward Willow Creek Station, feeling the coolness of the morning air fill his lungs. Each day in the forest felt like a new adventure, and he couldn't wait to see what he and Whistle would experience today.

When he arrived at the clearing, he found Whistle humming softly to himself, his headlights flickering warmly.

"Good morning, Whistle!" Toby greeted, giving the train an enthusiastic wave. "It's a perfect day for an adventure!"

"Good morning, Toby," Whistle replied cheerfully. "And I think you're right—today feels like a day for exploring. The forest seems especially lively today."

Just as Whistle finished speaking, a rustling sound came from a thicket of ferns near the edge of the clearing. Toby turned, curiosity piqued, and watched as a small, sleek figure emerged from the shadows. It was a fox, its reddish-brown fur glinting in the sunlight, and its bright, intelligent eyes scanning the clearing with a look of mischievous interest.

The fox trotted forward, stopping a few paces from Toby and Whistle, and then, to Toby's amazement, it spoke.

"Hello there! I don't think I've seen you around this part of the forest before," the fox said, his voice smooth and cheerful. He gave a little bow, as if introducing himself to old friends. "The name's Finn. I know this forest like the back of my paw."

Toby's eyes widened in delight. "You can talk? A talking fox?"

Finn grinned, his eyes twinkling with amusement. "Of course I can talk! Not many can understand me, though. You're a lucky one, Toby. I take it you're not new to magic?"

Toby glanced at Whistle with a grin, feeling a sense of pride. "Nope, not new at all. This is my friend Whistle, and he's the best train in the world."

Whistle let out a warm, welcoming hum. "Hello, Finn. It's a pleasure to meet you. I don't often get to talk to others in the forest."

Finn's ears perked up, and he trotted closer, sniffing at Whistle with keen interest. "A magical train! I've heard whispers about you. Some say you're as old as the trees, a guardian of forgotten tracks." He winked at Toby. "You have quite the friend here."

Toby felt his heart swell with excitement. "Finn, would you like to join us? We're always looking for new friends—and a guide who knows the forest would be amazing."

Finn's tail flicked with enthusiasm. "I'd be honoured! There's so much to see out here, and so many hidden places that most people pass right by. Stick with me, and I'll show you paths and secrets that only a fox would know."

Toby exchanged a delighted glance with Whistle, who let out a cheerful whistle in response. Finn clearly had a knack for adventure, and Toby couldn't wait to see what wonders lay hidden in the forest with Finn as their guide.

The three friends set off down a narrow path, with Finn trotting ahead, his nose twitching as he sniffed the air, always alert for interesting scents and sounds. The fox led them through winding trails, past towering oak trees and over small streams, each spot more enchanting than the last.

As they walked, Finn pointed out things that Toby would have missed on his own: a tiny family of mushrooms growing beneath a fallen log, a hidden hollow in a tree where squirrels stored acorns, and a patch of wildflowers that seemed to glow with an otherworldly light.

"See this moss?" Finn said, stopping by a tree with a thick coat of emerald-green moss. "It's not just any moss—if you touch it, it glows at night. They call it 'star moss.' The old forest folk say it has a touch of magic in it."

Toby reached out and gently touched the moss, feeling a soft tingle against his fingertips. He could hardly believe how much magic there was in the forest, all hidden in plain sight.

As they continued their walk, a light drizzle began to fall, sending tiny droplets glistening down from the leaves. The forest seemed to come alive even more, with the scent of damp earth and fresh rain filling the air.

Just then, Finn paused, his ears flicking back as he listened to something in the distance. "We're close to the Bluebell Glade," he whispered. "It's a secret spot where bluebells bloom year-round, and the ground is soft and springy. It's like walking on a carpet of flowers."

Toby's eyes widened in amazement. "That sounds beautiful! Lead the way, Finn!"

With a nod, Finn guided them through a dense patch of trees, and after a short walk, they emerged into a small clearing bathed in dappled sunlight. The ground was indeed covered in delicate bluebells, their soft petals swaying gently in the breeze. Toby felt like he'd stepped into a dream, and he couldn't help but smile at the beauty of it all.

"It's amazing, Finn," he said softly, feeling a deep sense of wonder. "Thank you for showing us this."

Finn gave a little bow, looking pleased. "I thought you'd like it. It's one of my favourite spots in the forest. There's a kind of peace here, a place where even the smallest creatures feel safe."

Toby sat down on the soft ground, surrounded by the bluebells, and closed his eyes for a moment, taking it all in. He felt connected to the forest, to Whistle, and to Finn, as if they were all part of something timeless and magical.

As he sat there, a question suddenly came to his mind. "Finn, why are you showing us all these places? I mean, you didn't have to..."

Finn's eyes softened, and he looked at Toby thoughtfully. "Because I can tell that you're a good friend, Toby. I can see it in the way you care for Whistle. The forest has a way of revealing its secrets to those who treat it with respect, and I can see that you do. It's rare to find someone who truly listens, and who sees magic in even the smallest things."

Toby felt a swell of gratitude and pride. "Thank you, Finn. I promise I'll always take care of the forest, and I'll keep its secrets safe."

Finn gave a nod, his tail flicking with satisfaction. "That's all the forest ever asks. And don't worry, I'll be here whenever you need a guide. Just look for me, and I'll find you."

The friends lingered a while longer in the Bluebell Glade, basking in the peace and beauty of the hidden spot. Toby felt as though he'd discovered a whole new world, one that only he, Whistle, and Finn shared. The forest had come alive in ways he'd never imagined, and he knew that these memories would stay with him forever.

As the sun began to dip lower in the sky, casting long shadows across the glade, Toby knew it was time to head back. He stood up, brushing off his pants, and turned to his friends.

"Thank you, Finn," he said warmly. "Today was... magical. I can't wait to explore more with you."

Finn gave him a toothy grin. "The pleasure's all mine, Toby. There's plenty more to see, and I'll be here to show you all of it."

With a final nod, Finn trotted off into the trees, his bushy tail disappearing into the shadows as swiftly as he had appeared. Toby and Whistle watched him go, their hearts filled with gratitude for their new friend.

As Toby climbed back onto Whistle and prepared to head home, he felt a deep sense of peace. The forest was now a place of secrets, wonders, and friends, and he knew that with Whistle and Finn by his side, every journey would be a new adventure.

As they rode back through the forest, Toby felt the magic of the day settle in his heart, a reminder of the friendship and trust he'd found.

With a smile, he leaned back and watched the trees pass by, knowing that he was part of a world filled with wonders he had only just begun to discover.

Chapter 12: A Journey to the Future

One crisp autumn morning, Toby arrived at Willow Creek Station, his mind buzzing with curiosity. His adventures with Whistle had opened his eyes to so many incredible things: a hidden world filled with magic, a friendship that spanned time, and now, a clever fox guide in Finn who seemed to know every secret of the forest. But today, as he approached Whistle, he could feel that something unusual was about to happen.

"Good morning, Whistle!" Toby called, giving his friend a wave.

"Good morning, Toby," Whistle replied warmly. "I've been thinking about our journeys together, and I realized that there's one more place I've yet to take you—a journey into a different time."

Toby's eyes widened with excitement. "Different time? Are we going back to the past again?"

Whistle's headlights flickered thoughtfully. "Not this time, Toby. Today, I'd like to show you the future. There are things you may need to understand about the world you're growing up in, things that only a glimpse of the future can teach you."

Toby felt a shiver of anticipation. He'd loved seeing his grandfather as a young boy during their last journey into the past, but the idea of seeing the future, of glimpsing the world he had yet to live in, filled him with a mix of excitement and curiosity.

"I'm ready, Whistle," he said, his voice filled with determination.

"Very well, then. Hold on tight," Whistle instructed, and Toby climbed onto the platform, settling into his usual spot. He took a deep breath as a familiar glow of light surrounded them, the forest fading away as they began their journey forward in time.

The light swirled around them, growing brighter and warmer until Toby had to close his eyes. When he opened them, he found himself standing in the same clearing, but it looked vastly different. The trees were taller, their trunks thicker and branches reaching high into the

TOBY AND THE TALKING TRAIN 53

sky. The air smelled faintly of flowers and fresh earth, and everything seemed sharper, more vibrant.

Toby looked around in awe. "This is... the future?"

Whistle let out a low hum. "Yes, Toby. But not just any future—this is a future shaped by the choices people make today."

Toby watched as a group of children ran through the clearing, laughing and playing, their voices echoing through the forest. They were carrying small, colorful devices in their hands that lit up with images and sounds, and their clothes looked like nothing Toby had ever seen before, made of bright, flexible materials that moved with them as they ran.

"They look so happy," Toby said, smiling as he watched the children play.

"Yes," Whistle replied. "This is a future where people have chosen to live in harmony with nature, where they've learned to respect the forest and use technology wisely. In this version of the future, people understand the importance of balance and kindness to the environment."

As they watched, one of the children paused to pick up a piece of litter, tossing it into a nearby bin that glowed and hummed, dissolving the litter instantly. The child grinned, proud of their small act, and joined the others in their game.

Toby felt a sense of pride watching them, but also a sense of responsibility. "So, if people make good choices now, this could be the future?"

Whistle let out a thoughtful hum. "Yes, Toby. But remember, choices have consequences, and not all choices lead to such a bright future."

With a gentle shift, the clearing began to blur and fade, and when it came back into focus, Toby found himself looking at a very different version of the forest. The trees were sparse, their trunks twisted and brittle, and the air felt thick and heavy, as though something was weighing it down. A dull grey haze hung over everything, dimming the sunlight and casting a shadow across the land.

Toby's heart sank as he took in the sight. The forest looked tired and sick, a mere shadow of the vibrant, living place he knew.

"What happened here?" he whispered, feeling a pang of sadness.

"This is another possible future," Whistle explained, his voice low and solemn. "In this version of the future, people didn't take care of the forest. They cut down too many trees, polluted the air, and didn't respect the delicate balance of nature. The forest could no longer thrive, and now it struggles to survive."

Toby felt a wave of sorrow as he gazed at the withered trees and the barren ground. The children he'd seen before were nowhere to be found, and the joyful sounds of laughter had been replaced by an eerie silence. He thought about the choices people were making today, choices that could lead to such a bleak future, and felt a weight settle on his heart.

"This is awful," he murmured. "I don't want this to be the future."

Whistle let out a soft hum. "And it doesn't have to be, Toby. The future is not set in stone. Every choice, no matter how small, can shape the path ahead. The way people treat nature, the way they care for each other—all of these choices create ripples that can lead to different outcomes."

Toby nodded, feeling a spark of determination. "Then I'll do everything I can to help make the better future happen. I'll make good choices and take care of the forest, and maybe I can help others see how important it is, too."

Whistle let out a warm, approving hum. "That's the spirit, Toby. Sometimes, it only takes one person to inspire others, to show them a different way. You have the power to make a difference."

The forest around them began to blur once more, and when the world came back into focus, Toby found himself back in the familiar clearing of Willow Creek Station, with the tall trees, soft moss, and gentle sounds of the forest filling the air.

He looked around, feeling a deep sense of gratitude for the world he had returned to. He understood now that this forest, this moment, was precious—and that it was up to him and everyone else to protect it.

"Thank you for showing me that, Whistle," Toby said quietly. "I didn't realize how much our choices mattered."

Whistle let out a gentle hum. "Sometimes, seeing the possibilities is the best way to understand the importance of our actions. You have a kind heart, Toby, and I know you'll make choices that lead to a bright future."

Toby nodded, a newfound resolve shining in his eyes. He thought about the children he'd seen in the first future, about their joy and the beauty of the thriving forest, and knew that he wanted to be part of a world like that.

As he prepared to leave Willow Creek Station, Toby felt a sense of purpose he hadn't felt before. He wanted to share what he'd learned, to inspire others to see the beauty of nature and the power of making good choices. He knew it wouldn't be easy, but with Whistle's lessons and the future he'd seen to guide him, he was ready to try.

With one last grateful look at Whistle, Toby set off down the path, the vision of a bright, green future filling his mind and heart. He felt as though he was carrying a spark of that future with him, a spark that he could help nurture and grow, one choice at a time.

Chapter 13: The Picnic Plan

The air was crisp and fresh, filled with the earthy scent of fallen leaves and the soft warmth of the autumn sun. Toby arrived at Willow Creek Station with a special plan in mind. He'd been thinking about all the new friends he and Whistle had made—Finn the fox, the squirrels and birds they often encountered, and even the shy deer that sometimes wandered near the clearing. Today, Toby wanted to do something special to celebrate these friendships and enjoy the magic of the forest together.

"Good morning, Whistle!" Toby greeted, bouncing with excitement.

"Good morning, Toby," Whistle replied warmly. "You seem to be brimming with energy. Do you have something in mind?"

Toby grinned, unable to hold back his enthusiasm. "I was thinking... what if we have a picnic? We could invite our animal friends, have some treats, and just enjoy the day together. It'll be a celebration of friendship!"

Whistle let out a pleased hum. "That sounds like a wonderful idea, Toby. A picnic would be a delightful way to spend the day—and to show our friends how much we appreciate them."

With Whistle's encouragement, Toby started planning. He had brought a basket filled with snacks he thought everyone would enjoy: berries and nuts for the animals, and some sandwiches, apple slices, and cookies he'd made with his mom the day before. The basket was brimming with treats, and Toby felt proud knowing he'd have something for everyone.

As they set up the picnic area in a sunlit patch near the station, Toby couldn't help but feel a growing sense of excitement. The blanket was spread, the food arranged neatly, and Whistle gave a cheerful whistle to announce the start of the picnic.

TOBY AND THE TALKING TRAIN

Within moments, a rustling came from the nearby bushes, and Finn appeared, his nose twitching as he caught the delicious scents wafting from the blanket.

"A picnic! Now that's an idea I can get behind!" Finn exclaimed, his eyes twinkling with excitement as he trotted over and took a seat beside Toby. "I smell berries... and, is that fresh bread?"

Toby laughed, handing Finn a handful of berries. "I knew you'd be the first to arrive, Finn. You've got a nose for food!"

Finn grinned, munching happily on the berries. "You've got me figured out, Toby. Nothing gets past this nose!"

One by one, other animals began to arrive. A family of squirrels skittered down from a nearby tree, their eyes wide with curiosity as they scurried over to the blanket. Toby smiled, offering them a handful of nuts, which they accepted eagerly, chattering happily as they nibbled on their treats.

A couple of birds swooped down, perching on the edge of the blanket as Toby offered them small pieces of apple. They chirped in appreciation, their bright feathers gleaming in the sunlight. Even a shy deer cautiously approached, its gentle eyes watching Toby as he extended some apple slices. The deer accepted the treat with a delicate nod, munching contentedly.

Toby felt his heart swell with happiness as he watched his animal friends enjoy the treats. There was something magical about sharing with others, about creating a moment of joy that everyone could experience together.

Whistle let out a soft hum, watching the scene with warmth and pride. "It's wonderful to see everyone here, Toby. You've created a moment of togetherness, one that reminds us all of the beauty of sharing."

Toby smiled, realizing how true Whistle's words were. The animals were his friends, and this picnic felt like a way to celebrate their bond, to show them kindness and gratitude for the companionship they'd shared.

As they enjoyed their picnic, Finn stretched out lazily, sighing with contentment. "Nothing like a feast with friends to make a day complete," he said, looking up at Toby with a grateful smile. "You know, Toby, not many humans think to share like this. Most of them keep to themselves, but you... you're different."

Toby felt a surge of pride at Finn's words. "Thanks, Finn. I just wanted everyone to know how much I appreciate them. I think the forest is more magical because of you all."

One of the squirrels, emboldened by Toby's kindness, darted over and nuzzled his hand, chirping happily before scampering back to its family. The small gesture filled Toby with warmth, a reminder that even the smallest acts of sharing and kindness could bring happiness.

As the afternoon wore on, they laughed, shared stories, and basked in the warmth of the sun. Toby learned from Finn about hidden trails in the forest, listened to the squirrels' playful chatter, and enjoyed the peaceful presence of the deer and birds around them. It was a gathering unlike any other, and Toby realized how special it was to share these moments.

At one point, Whistle spoke up, his voice carrying a note of gentle wisdom. "Toby, sharing is one of the greatest ways we can connect with others. It shows trust, kindness, and a willingness to give a part of ourselves. By sharing this day with your friends, you've brought happiness to each of them."

Toby nodded, understanding more deeply. "I guess sharing is like a gift, one that keeps giving back. When we share, we're not just giving something away—we're creating memories, connections."

The animals seemed to understand Toby's words, each of them chirping, chattering, or nodding in agreement. It was as though they, too, felt the joy and beauty of this shared moment, one that would linger in their memories long after the picnic ended.

TOBY AND THE TALKING TRAIN

As the sun began to dip lower in the sky, casting a warm, golden glow over the clearing, Toby knew it was time to start packing up. He gathered the remains of the picnic, sharing the last few treats with his friends before tucking the empty basket under his arm.

Finn gave a playful bow, his tail flicking with joy. "Thank you, Toby. This was a feast fit for a fox—and a day I won't soon forget."

The squirrels chattered their thanks, the birds chirped in appreciation, and even the deer gave a gentle nod before disappearing into the trees. Toby watched them go, his heart full of joy, knowing that they had all shared something truly special.

As he climbed back onto the platform beside Whistle, he looked back at the clearing, feeling a deep sense of peace.

"Thank you for helping me, Whistle," he said, patting the side of the train. "I couldn't have done it without you."

Whistle let out a soft, contented hum. "You're very welcome, Toby. Today, you showed your friends the kindness in your heart. And kindness, like a picnic, is always best enjoyed when shared."

Toby smiled, feeling the truth of Whistle's words settle within him. He had learned that sharing wasn't just about giving away things—it was about creating moments of happiness, building bonds, and filling the world with kindness.

As he made his way home, Toby carried the warmth of the day with him, knowing that his friendships with Whistle and the forest creatures had grown stronger. He felt grateful for each of them, and he knew that their shared memories would stay with him forever.

And as he walked down the familiar path, he realized that this was only the beginning. There would be more adventures, more moments to share, and more friendships to cherish—all made richer by the joy of giving and connecting with others.

Chapter 14: The Puzzle at Midnight

It was a clear, chilly evening, and Toby had settled into bed, expecting a quiet night of sleep. Just as he was drifting off, a soft whistle echoed through the air, barely audible over the quiet hum of the night. Toby sat up, recognizing the sound immediately—it was Whistle, calling him. He threw on his jacket, grabbed a flashlight, and tiptoed quietly out of the house, excitement building in his chest. Midnight visits to Willow Creek Station were rare, and he couldn't help but wonder what Whistle had planned.

When he arrived at the clearing, the moonlight cast a silvery glow over the station, making everything look a little magical. Whistle waited for him, headlights dim but welcoming, as if holding a secret just for Toby.

"Hello, Whistle!" Toby whispered, feeling the thrill of the late-night adventure. "You called?"

"Good evening, Toby," Whistle replied in a low, mysterious hum. "Tonight, I have something special for you. I've been thinking about how much you've learned on our adventures, and I believe you're ready for a challenge—a riddle that requires both creativity and trust in yourself."

Toby's eyes lit up. He loved riddles and puzzles, and he knew Whistle wouldn't make it easy. "I'm ready! What's the riddle?"

Whistle let out a gentle chuckle. "Very well, here it is. Listen closely, Toby, because this riddle is unique. It's not just about finding an answer—it's about uncovering a journey."

Toby leaned in, focused, as Whistle began.

"I am not seen in daylight, yet I light up the night.
I hide in the forest, not in plain sight.
To find me, Toby, follow your heart,
For I am a piece of magic, a forest-born spark."

Toby repeated the riddle to himself, letting each line sink in. "Not seen in daylight... lights up the night... hides in the forest." His mind raced with ideas, but nothing immediately felt right. He knew Whistle well enough to understand that this wouldn't be a straightforward answer—it was likely something magical, something hidden.

Whistle watched him thoughtfully. "This is a journey as much as it is a puzzle, Toby. Follow your instincts, and trust yourself."

Toby took a deep breath, letting the words echo in his mind. "A piece of magic, a forest-born spark," he murmured to himself. "That sounds almost like... a firefly? But no, it's late autumn. Fireflies aren't out this time of year."

He thought harder. The answer had to be something more subtle, something that wasn't immediately visible in daylight but appeared at night. Then he remembered Finn, the fox, mentioning something about star moss—a glowing moss hidden in certain parts of the forest.

"Could it be the star moss?" Toby asked, looking at Whistle for confirmation.

Whistle let out a soft, encouraging hum but didn't confirm or deny it. "You're on the right path, Toby. Sometimes, it's not about the answer but the journey to it. Trust your instincts."

Toby nodded, feeling his excitement grow as he turned toward the forest. He switched on his flashlight and stepped carefully into the trees, letting his memory guide him toward the places where he'd seen the moss before. The forest felt different at night—more mysterious, with shadows stretching and shifting in the moonlight. But instead of feeling scared, Toby felt a sense of purpose, as though the forest were guiding him.

He walked for a while, listening to the sounds of the night: the rustling leaves, the distant hoot of an owl, the soft crunch of leaves underfoot. His mind kept returning to the riddle, repeating the lines like a mantra.

Just when he started to wonder if he was on the right track, he spotted a faint glow ahead, nestled against the base of an ancient tree. He moved closer, and sure enough, a patch of star moss lay there, casting a soft, greenish glow. It wasn't bright enough to be seen from far away, but up close, it looked like tiny stars twinkling on the forest floor.

Toby's heart leapt with excitement. "This must be it!"

But as he approached the moss, he realized there was something even more mysterious. A small, delicate box lay half-buried in the moss, its silver surface reflecting the faint glow of the star moss around it. Toby carefully picked it up, feeling a thrill of discovery. The box was old, with intricate carvings of vines and stars etched into its lid.

With a deep breath, he opened the lid, revealing a tiny silver key and a folded piece of paper inside. He took out the paper and unfolded it, revealing a note in neat, flowing handwriting:

"A key to the heart of magic lies in your hands. For the next step, trust where you began."

Toby reread the note, trying to make sense of it. "The heart of magic... trust where I began..." He thought back to the riddle and everything he'd learned in the forest with Whistle. The answer must be somewhere close to where he had first met Whistle—Willow Creek Station.

He tucked the key into his pocket, carefully closed the box, and made his way back to Whistle, his heart racing with excitement.

When he returned to the station, Whistle was waiting for him with a soft, knowing hum. "Did you find what you were looking for, Toby?"

Toby nodded, holding up the silver key. "I found this! And the note says the next step is where I began... I think it must be here, at Willow Creek Station."

Whistle let out a gentle, approving whistle. "You're indeed correct. Now, there's one final step. This key belongs to something hidden beneath the platform—a treasure that has waited a long time to be discovered. You must unlock it with both the key and your heart."

Toby's eyes widened as he knelt down beside the platform, feeling along the wooden boards until his fingers brushed against a hidden compartment. He slid the silver key into a tiny lock, and with a soft click, the compartment opened, revealing a small leather-bound book with a shimmering, star-like pattern on its cover.

The book felt warm and alive in his hands, as though it held stories and secrets waiting just for him.

"Go ahead, Toby. Open it," Whistle urged.

Toby opened the book carefully, flipping through pages filled with delicate, hand-drawn maps of the forest, tales of past Listeners who had once befriended magical trains, and notes on magical places hidden throughout the woods. It was a guidebook, a treasure trove of knowledge about the enchanted forest and the special connection between the Listeners and the forest's magic.

Toby's eyes shone with wonder as he read snippets of tales and descriptions of places he had yet to explore. He realized that this was more than a simple book—it was a record of those who had come before him, those who had shared a friendship with Whistle and the forest's magic.

He looked up at Whistle, his voice filled with awe. "This... this is amazing. It's like I'm part of something bigger than I ever imagined."

Whistle let out a soft hum, his headlights glowing warmly. "You are, Toby. You're part of a legacy, a tradition of friendship, trust, and wonder. This book is a gift to help guide you on your journey, to encourage you to think beyond what you see and trust in the magic of your own heart."

Toby closed the book gently, feeling a surge of gratitude. The puzzle had been more than just a test—it had been a way for him to discover a new part of himself, to realize that he had the courage and curiosity to uncover the mysteries of the world around him.

"Thank you, Whistle," Toby said, his voice full of emotion. "This was the best puzzle I've ever solved. And I promise, I'll honour the stories in this book and carry on the legacy of the Listeners."

Whistle gave a low, contented whistle. "I know you will, Toby. The forest has found a true friend in you."

As Toby made his way back home, the book clutched tightly in his hands, he felt a newfound sense of purpose. The riddle had not only challenged his mind but had also taught him to trust in himself, in his instincts, and in the magic that lay within his heart.

With a heart full of gratitude, Toby knew that his journey was only just beginning—and that, with Whistle and the forest as his guides, there was no limit to the wonders he would uncover.

Chapter 15: A Lesson in Forgiveness

One crisp autumn afternoon, Toby arrived at Willow Creek Station feeling more excited than usual. He was in the middle of reading the magical guidebook Whistle had given him during their last adventure, and each page filled him with wonder and new ideas for their future journeys together. In his excitement, he had packed a few small tools and trinkets he thought might be useful—things he'd found around the house, like a small flashlight, an old compass, and even a screwdriver in case anything needed fixing.

When he reached Whistle, he immediately shared his enthusiasm. "Good afternoon, Whistle! I brought some tools with me today. I thought maybe we could go on a new kind of adventure, or maybe even explore the compartments under your engine!"

Whistle let out a warm hum. "That sounds wonderful, Toby. Curiosity is always a good companion for adventures. But remember, I have some delicate parts, so we'll have to be careful."

Toby nodded, barely containing his excitement. He started by exploring the outside of Whistle, looking over every detail he could. Soon, his eyes landed on a panel near Whistle's engine that he hadn't noticed before, one that seemed to be slightly ajar. Without thinking too much, he took out his screwdriver, hoping to open it further and see what was inside.

He wedged the screwdriver into the small gap, trying to pry the panel open. But as he pressed harder, the screwdriver slipped, and with a loud clank, the metal scratched the side of Whistle's engine. Toby froze, staring at the long scratch that now marred Whistle's side. He hadn't meant to damage anything—he was only trying to look inside.

"Oh no..." Toby whispered, a feeling of dread settling over him. He looked at the scratch, guilt twisting his stomach. He hadn't listened when Whistle had said to be careful. How could he have been so careless?

Whistle was silent for a moment, his headlights dimmer than usual. Finally, he let out a low, sad hum. "Toby... I know you didn't mean to harm me, but I am a bit hurt. That panel is one of my oldest parts, and it holds memories of my journeys."

Toby's heart sank. He wanted nothing more than to undo the scratch, to make things right, but he didn't know how. "I'm so sorry, Whistle," he said, his voice filled with regret. "I just... I got too excited. I wasn't thinking."

Whistle let out a gentle, understanding hum, but Toby could feel the sadness lingering in his friend's voice. "I know you didn't mean it, Toby. But even accidents can have consequences. Sometimes, when we're too eager, we forget to take the care we should."

Toby nodded, feeling tears prick at his eyes. He took a deep breath, trying to steady himself. He knew he had to make this right, somehow. But it would take more than just an apology; he needed to show Whistle that he understood the importance of being careful, of respecting his friend's boundaries.

"Whistle, I promise I'll be more careful from now on," Toby said earnestly. "I'll never try to open something on you without asking first. And... I want to make it up to you. Maybe I could clean your panels, or polish them to make them shine again?"

Whistle let out a gentle, forgiving hum, and Toby felt a wave of relief wash over him. "Thank you for your apology, Toby. It takes courage to admit when we've made a mistake. And I would appreciate a bit of polishing. It would show me that you care."

The two friends sat together in a comfortable silence as Toby considered what he could do to make Whistle feel better. After a moment, he reached into his backpack and pulled out a soft cloth he'd brought for cleaning his flashlight. Gently, he began polishing Whistle's panels, moving slowly and carefully, trying to buff out the scratch he had caused.

As he worked, Toby thought about the importance of being mindful with his actions. He realized that Whistle wasn't just any train—he was a friend who deserved respect and care. This scratch, though small, was a reminder of how easily things could go wrong if he wasn't careful.

As he polished, Whistle's voice grew softer and warmer. "Thank you, Toby. I can feel that you're taking your time, and that means a great deal to me. Apologies are important, but making amends shows true understanding."

Toby looked up, his eyes filled with sincerity. "I really am sorry, Whistle. I should have listened when you told me to be careful. I'll always remember this, and I'll never take you for granted again."

They stayed together, Toby polishing Whistle's panels until they shone brightly in the late afternoon sunlight. The scratch, though still faintly visible, was softened by Toby's careful attention, and Toby felt a sense of accomplishment, knowing he had done his best to repair the mistake.

After a while, Whistle let out a cheerful hum, his headlights glowing a bit brighter. "There, all polished and feeling much better. Thank you, Toby. You've shown me that you truly care, and that means more than any repair."

Toby smiled, feeling a weight lift from his heart. He realized that Whistle's forgiveness was a gift, one that he would treasure. "Thank you for forgiving me, Whistle. I'll always remember this lesson."

As the sun began to set, Toby prepared to head home, feeling a sense of peace and gratitude. He knew that this experience would stay with him, a reminder that even small actions had consequences, and that true friendship meant being willing to admit mistakes and make things right.

And as he walked back through the forest, he felt a renewed sense of respect for his friend, knowing that forgiveness, like trust, was something precious that needed to be earned and cherished.

The scratch might remain, a faint mark on Whistle's side, but to Toby, it was a reminder of the lesson he'd learned and the bond he shared with his friend—a bond built on trust, understanding, and the power of making amends.

Chapter 16: Meeting the Owl of Wisdom

It was a quiet evening in the forest, the kind of night where even the leaves seemed to whisper secrets to each other. Toby made his way to Willow Creek Station, the light of his flashlight casting a soft glow on the path ahead. After the lesson he'd learned about forgiveness with Whistle, he felt even closer to his friend, and he was eager for another adventure.

When he arrived, Whistle greeted him with a warm hum. "Good evening, Toby. Tonight, I have someone special for you to meet."

Toby's curiosity was piqued. "Who is it?"

Whistle's headlights flickered softly, as if in a knowing smile. "An old friend of mine—a wise soul who has been in this forest for many, many years. He has watched generations come and go, seen the seasons change, and carries a wealth of wisdom. He is known as the Owl of Wisdom."

Toby's eyes widened. An owl? He had always thought of owls as mysterious creatures, wise and silent, perched high in the trees. "I'd love to meet him! What kind of wisdom does he have?"

Whistle let out a gentle hum. "Patience, young Listener. Wisdom is best gathered slowly, just like the night settles over the forest. He'll be here soon."

As if on cue, a soft, low hoot echoed through the trees. Toby looked up, and in the moonlight, he saw a large owl gliding silently toward them, his wings barely making a sound as he descended. The owl's feathers were a mixture of greys and browns, blending perfectly with the shadows of the forest, and his golden eyes shone with a quiet intelligence.

The owl landed gracefully on a branch near Whistle, gazing down at Toby with a calm and steady look. Toby felt a strange, comforting sensation in the owl's presence, as if he were looking at someone who had all the answers and was content to share them slowly, in due time.

"Hello, young one," the owl said, his voice soft and smooth, like a gentle breeze through the trees. "I am Eldric, the Owl of Wisdom."

Toby gave a respectful nod. "Hello, Eldric. It's an honour to meet you."

Eldric inclined his head, his keen gaze fixed on Toby. "I have been watching you, young Listener. Whistle speaks highly of you, and I see that you carry a thoughtful spirit. But every journey, even one filled with curiosity, needs wisdom."

Toby nodded, feeling both humbled and excited to hear Eldric's words. "I'd love to learn, Eldric. How can I make wise choices?"

Eldric's eyes gleamed. "Wisdom, young one, is not a single answer but rather a way of approaching life. It means understanding that every choice carries a consequence, and considering not only what you want, but what others need as well."

Toby listened carefully, letting Eldric's words settle in his mind. He thought back to his recent experience with Whistle, remembering how his eagerness had led to a mistake. He had learned from it, but he realized that he hadn't considered the consequences of his actions until it was too late.

Eldric continued, his voice calm and thoughtful. "When you face a choice, ask yourself three questions: Will this choice harm anyone? Does it honour the truth? And will it bring kindness into the world?"

Toby repeated the questions to himself, feeling their weight and simplicity. "Will this choice harm anyone? Does it honour the truth? And will it bring kindness..."

The owl nodded approvingly. "By asking these questions, you allow yourself to pause and consider the path ahead, rather than rushing forward blindly. True wisdom lies in patience and understanding, in seeing beyond what's right in front of you."

Toby glanced at Whistle, who was watching quietly, his headlights glowing gently. Whistle had often taught him similar lessons—about patience, kindness, and the importance of thinking before acting. But hearing it from Eldric felt like another layer of understanding, a reminder that wisdom was a lifelong journey.

"Can I ask you something, Eldric?" Toby said, looking up at the owl.

Eldric nodded, his golden eyes twinkling. "Of course, young one. A wise question is always welcome."

"What if... what if I make a choice and it turns out to be the wrong one, even if I try to be wise?" Toby asked, voicing the worry that had lingered in his mind since his mistake with Whistle.

Eldric gazed at him with gentle understanding. "Mistakes, Toby, are a part of learning. Even the wisest make them. The key is to take responsibility for those mistakes, to seek forgiveness if needed, and to learn so that you choose differently next time."

Whistle let out a soft hum, as if in agreement. "Remember, Toby, that wisdom grows with experience. Each choice, whether right or wrong, is a step on the path to understanding."

Toby felt a surge of relief. He realized that wisdom didn't mean being perfect; it meant being thoughtful, open to learning, and willing to grow. He looked up at Eldric, feeling a deep sense of gratitude. "Thank you, Eldric. I'll remember your advice. I'll try to make choices that don't hurt anyone, that are honest, and that bring kindness into the world."

Eldric gave a wise nod, his feathers ruffling slightly in the cool night breeze. "Then you are already on the path of wisdom, Toby. Remember, true wisdom is not a destination but a journey. And I believe you will walk that path with honour."

The owl lifted his wings, preparing to take flight. Before he did, he cast a final look at Toby, his golden eyes filled with encouragement. "We may meet again, young Listener, when the time is right. For now, carry my words with you."

With a powerful beat of his wings, Eldric soared into the sky, disappearing into the shadows of the trees as silently as he had come.

Toby watched him go, feeling as though he had just glimpsed a piece of ancient magic, a reminder of the quiet wisdom that the forest held.

As he turned to Whistle, Toby felt a sense of peace and purpose. "I'll remember Eldric's words, Whistle. I'll do my best to make wise choices, and to think before I act."

Whistle gave a contented hum, his headlights glowing warmly. "I know you will, Toby. Wisdom is a lifelong friend, one that grows with you, and I believe you are well on your way."

With a heart full of gratitude, Toby said goodbye to Whistle and made his way back through the forest, Eldric's questions echoing in his mind. Will this choice harm anyone? Does it honour the truth? And will it bring kindness into the world?

He knew that he wouldn't always have the answers, but he was ready to try his best, to think carefully, and to approach each choice with kindness. As he walked under the silver light of the moon, he felt a new strength within him—a quiet, steady wisdom that would guide him on his journey.

And with Eldric's words in his heart, Toby knew that he was ready for whatever choices and adventures lay ahead.

Chapter 17: Toby's First Big Mistake

The morning was bright and cheerful as Toby made his way to school, his thoughts drifting back to his adventures with Whistle and the wise words of Eldric, the Owl of Wisdom. He felt a sense of confidence in himself—he had learned so much about friendship, kindness, and the importance of making wise choices. But little did he know, today he would face a lesson of his own making, one that would test everything he had learned.

During lunch, Toby's best friend Leo sat beside him, talking excitedly about their plans for the weekend. Toby smiled, nodding along, but his mind kept wandering back to Willow Creek Station and Whistle. His adventures with Whistle had become such a huge part of his life, and he often found himself wanting to share it with someone. But he remembered Whistle's warning: their friendship was a special secret, a magic that only he and a few trusted friends of the forest shared.

Just then, Leo turned to him, eyes bright with curiosity. "Hey, Toby, you've been acting a bit different lately. You're always sneaking off to the woods by yourself. What's going on?"

Toby felt his stomach tighten. He wanted to keep Whistle's secret, but he also wanted to be honest with his friend. The temptation to share his adventures grew stronger as he looked at Leo, his best friend, someone he had trusted with everything up until now.

"Uh... it's nothing," Toby mumbled, but the words felt hollow even as he said them.

Leo frowned, looking hurt. "Come on, Toby. I thought we told each other everything. What's so important out there that you can't tell me?"

Toby's resolve wavered. He didn't want Leo to feel left out, and he certainly didn't want to lose his friend's trust. After a moment of hesitation, the words slipped out before he could stop them.

"Alright... I'll tell you," he said quietly, glancing around to make sure no one else was listening. He took a deep breath and, lowering his voice, began to tell Leo about Whistle, the magical train hidden in the forest, and the adventures they'd shared.

Leo's eyes widened in disbelief, then excitement. "A talking train? In the woods? That's incredible! Can I meet him?"

Realizing what he had done, Toby felt a wave of guilt wash over him. He had just broken his promise to Whistle, revealing a secret he'd been entrusted to protect. But Leo looked so excited that Toby pushed the feeling aside, hoping it wouldn't be a big deal.

"Maybe," he said hesitantly. "But you have to keep it a secret, okay? Nobody else can know."

Leo grinned, nodding eagerly. "I promise, Toby! I won't tell anyone."

But as the day went on, Toby's excitement began to fade, replaced by a growing sense of dread. He had broken his promise to Whistle, revealing a secret that wasn't his to share. The words of Eldric came back to him, reminding him of the importance of making choices that honoured trust and kindness.

By the time he made his way to Willow Creek Station that evening, his heart was heavy with guilt. When he reached the clearing, Whistle was waiting, his headlights glowing softly in the dimming light.

"Hello, Toby," Whistle greeted, but there was a hint of concern in his voice. "You look troubled. Is everything alright?"

Toby took a deep breath, feeling a lump rise in his throat. He knew he couldn't hide the truth from Whistle, not after everything they had been through. "Whistle, I... I made a mistake. A big one."

Whistle let out a gentle, patient hum, waiting for Toby to continue.

"I told Leo about you," Toby admitted, his voice barely a whisper. "I know I shouldn't have. I broke my promise. I just... I didn't want him to feel left out. And now, I feel terrible."

TOBY AND THE TALKING TRAIN

There was a long silence as Whistle absorbed Toby's words. Finally, Whistle spoke, his voice calm but tinged with sadness. "Trust is a delicate thing, Toby. Once broken, it takes effort to repair. I shared my secret with you because I trusted you to keep it safe. But I also know that everyone makes mistakes, and what matters is what you do to make things right."

Toby nodded, feeling a wave of relief that Whistle was willing to give him a chance to fix his mistake. "I'm so sorry, Whistle. I should have thought about what it would mean to share your secret. Is there any way I can make it up to you?"

Whistle let out a thoughtful hum. "Making amends isn't always easy, Toby, but it begins with honesty. You must talk to Leo and explain why it's important to keep this a secret. And remember, it's not enough to just apologize; you must show through your actions that you understand the importance of trust."

The next day at school, Toby found Leo during lunch, his heart pounding with nerves. "Leo, I need to talk to you," he began, his voice serious.

Leo looked at him with concern. "What's up, Toby?"

Toby took a deep breath, gathering his courage. "I need to ask you to keep what I told you about Whistle a complete secret. I wasn't supposed to tell anyone, and I shouldn't have told you, even though you're my best friend. I made a mistake, and I need you to help me make it right by keeping it between us."

Leo looked at Toby, surprised by his sincerity. "I get it, Toby, I'll keep it a secret, I promise. I'm sorry if I pressured you into telling me."

Toby felt a weight lift from his shoulders. "Thank you, Leo. I just really want to keep Whistle's trust. It's important to me."

That evening, Toby returned to Willow Creek Station, feeling a sense of peace after his conversation with Leo. When he arrived, he found Whistle waiting, his headlights glowing softly in the twilight.

"I spoke to Leo, Whistle," Toby said. "I told him why it was important to keep your secret, and he promised he wouldn't tell anyone. I know it doesn't undo my mistake, but I'll do my best to earn back your trust."

Whistle let out a warm, forgiving hum. "Thank you, Toby. I can see that you understand the importance of honesty and making things right. Trust isn't about never making mistakes—it's about being willing to admit them and learning from them."

Toby felt a deep sense of gratitude for Whistle's understanding. "I promise, I'll never take your trust for granted again."

As they sat together in the quiet of the forest, Toby reflected on the lessons he had learned. He realized that honesty wasn't just about telling the truth—it was about respecting the trust others placed in him, and knowing when to keep something private, even from those closest to him.

In the fading light, he looked at Whistle with renewed respect and gratitude. This journey had taught him that mistakes could be powerful teachers, and that sometimes, making things right meant more than any adventure.

With a final, thankful pat on Whistle's side, Toby headed home, feeling the strength of the lesson he had learned settle within him. He knew that honesty and trust were gifts—gifts he would work hard to protect, now and always.

Chapter 18: The Train That Lost Its Voice

The first frost had settled over the forest, giving everything a crisp, silvery sheen. Toby made his way through the woods to Willow Creek Station, excited to see Whistle and eager to share a new story he'd found in the magical guidebook. But as he approached the clearing, he noticed something unusual. The air was strangely silent—no familiar hum or gentle whistle greeted him.

"Whistle?" Toby called out, concern creeping into his voice.

Whistle's headlights flickered on, but instead of his usual warm greeting, only a faint, struggling sound came from the engine. It was as if he was trying to speak but couldn't find his voice. Toby's heart sank.

"Whistle, are you alright?" Toby asked, moving closer, his hand resting on the side of his friend.

Whistle let out a soft, static-like crackle, but still, no words came. Toby felt a pang of worry—it was clear that something was wrong. He had never seen Whistle so quiet, and he realized how much he depended on his friend's comforting voice.

"I'm here, Whistle," Toby said softly, hoping his presence could bring some comfort. "I don't know what's happened, but I'll do everything I can to help you."

Whistle flickered his headlights in what Toby understood to be gratitude. Despite his concern, Toby felt a surge of determination. He couldn't imagine the forest without Whistle's voice, and he knew he had to find a way to help his friend.

He remembered the wise words of Eldric, the Owl of Wisdom, about listening carefully and thinking before acting. With these lessons in mind, Toby decided to start by investigating what could be causing Whistle's silence.

"Let's start by checking around your engine," Toby said gently. "Maybe there's something caught in the gears or blocking your voice."

Toby moved around Whistle, carefully inspecting every panel and joint. He looked for anything that might be causing the problem, but everything seemed as it should be. Frustrated but undeterred, he thought of other ways he could help. He remembered that Whistle's voice wasn't just mechanical—it was also magical.

He realized he would need help from someone who understood the magic of the forest better than he did.

With a sense of purpose, Toby went to find Finn, the clever fox who always seemed to know more about the forest than anyone else. After a short search, he found Finn lounging near a hollow log, grooming his tail.

"Finn! I need your help," Toby said breathlessly.

Finn looked up, his eyes sharp with curiosity. "Well, well, if it isn't my friend Toby. What's got you all in a rush?"

"It's Whistle. He's... he's lost his voice, and I don't know how to help him," Toby explained. "Do you know anything about why this might happen?"

Finn's ears perked up, and he nodded thoughtfully. "Ah, the voice of a magical train is a delicate thing, Toby. It's tied not just to its parts, but to its spirit. Sometimes, a train's voice can be affected by things it feels—just like how you might lose your words when you're upset."

Toby's eyes widened as he thought about this. "So... maybe Whistle lost his voice because something's bothering him?"

Finn nodded. "Could be. Maybe he's feeling unwell or troubled by something he hasn't shared. Magical trains, like any friend, need care and attention beyond just fixing parts."

Toby thought carefully, remembering the times Whistle had comforted him. He realized that he had never stopped to think about how Whistle might be feeling. He had always seen Whistle as his wise, unbreakable friend. But now he understood that even the strongest friends could feel vulnerable.

TOBY AND THE TALKING TRAIN 79

"Thanks, Finn," Toby said gratefully. "I'll go back and let Whistle know I'm here for him, no matter what. Maybe... maybe that's all he needs."

Returning to Willow Creek Station, Toby sat beside Whistle, feeling a wave of empathy and compassion for his friend. He gently placed his hand on Whistle's side and spoke softly.

"Whistle, I didn't realize that you might be feeling... well, anything like worry or sadness. I've always thought of you as my wise, strong friend, someone I could turn to for help. But I guess I never stopped to think that maybe you need someone to listen to you, too."

Whistle's headlights flickered, and Toby could feel a faint vibration, as if Whistle were responding to his words. Though Whistle couldn't speak, Toby sensed that his friend was trying to communicate, expressing his gratitude for Toby's presence.

Toby sat with Whistle in comfortable silence, the kind that only close friends share. He spoke softly about their adventures, recalling the time they had met Conductor Clara, their visit to the future, and their magical picnic in the forest. As he reminisced, he could feel Whistle's spirit lifting, as though his friend was remembering these moments fondly.

Finally, Toby took a deep breath and said, "Whistle, I don't need you to be perfect or always strong. I just need you to be here with me. Whatever you're going through, I'm here for you, just like you've always been there for me."

In that moment, a soft hum began to vibrate through Whistle's engine, faint at first, then slowly growing stronger. Toby's heart leapt as he realized that Whistle's voice was returning.

"Toby..." Whistle's voice was quiet, a little scratchy, but it was there. "Thank you. I didn't know how to tell you I was feeling... weary. I feared losing my voice meant I was losing my purpose."

Toby felt a wave of emotion as he listened. "You're not losing your purpose, Whistle. You mean the world to me, voice or no voice. And if you ever feel this way again, you can always share it with me. You've taught me so much—now let me be here for you, too."

With a warm hum, Whistle's voice grew clearer and more confident. "You've shown me kindness beyond words, Toby. Sometimes, even the strongest hearts need a friend to remind them they're not alone."

As they sat together under the growing moonlight, Toby felt a new depth to his friendship with Whistle. He had always seen Whistle as a source of wisdom, but now he understood that even those who seem the wisest have feelings and vulnerabilities, too. They need understanding, empathy, and, most importantly, the reassurance of a friend who will stand by them.

Toby stayed by Whistle's side long into the night, sharing memories, listening, and letting his friend know he was cherished. He knew now that being a friend meant being there through both joy and difficulty, and he was grateful to have the chance to show Whistle just how much he cared.

As he finally made his way home, Toby's heart was full, knowing that he and Whistle had grown closer than ever. The forest was quiet, and the stars shone brightly above, as if they, too, understood the importance of friendship, empathy, and the quiet strength that comes from simply being there for one another.

Chapter 19: The Golden Ticket

It was an ordinary day in the forest, the air filled with the earthy scent of fallen leaves and the rustling of branches in the gentle breeze. Toby was on his usual path to Willow Creek Station, lost in thought as he remembered his latest adventure with Whistle. Their friendship had deepened in ways he hadn't imagined, and each day felt like a new chapter in their story together.

As he walked, something shiny caught his eye. Toby stopped and knelt down, brushing aside a few leaves to reveal a small, gleaming ticket lying on the forest floor. The ticket was unlike anything he'd ever seen—golden, with swirling, intricate designs etched along the edges, and a faint shimmer that seemed to change in the sunlight.

Toby carefully picked up the ticket, his heart pounding with excitement. He examined it closely, noticing delicate script written across the top:

"The Golden Ticket: Admit One to a Special Adventure."

Below the text, he saw a small note written in elegant handwriting: "To find your way, follow the light at the end of the day."

Toby's mind raced. A special adventure? And a mysterious ticket that had appeared out of nowhere? He felt a thrill of curiosity and wonder, knowing this must be something magical. Without another thought, he hurried to Willow Creek Station, eager to share his discovery with Whistle.

When he arrived, Whistle was waiting, his headlights glowing softly as if he'd sensed Toby's excitement.

"Whistle! Look what I found!" Toby called out, holding up the golden ticket.

Whistle hummed with interest as Toby showed him the ticket. "Well, well... a golden ticket. I haven't seen one of these in years. They're quite rare, you know."

"What is it for?" Toby asked, his eyes shining with anticipation.

Whistle let out a soft chuckle. "Golden tickets are magical invitations, Toby. They lead their finder to a unique adventure, one that holds a special lesson or discovery. But each ticket has its own mystery—you'll need to follow its clues to uncover what lies ahead."

Toby glanced at the ticket again, rereading the clue: "To find your way, follow the light at the end of the day."

"So... it means I need to go somewhere at sunset?" Toby guessed, looking up at Whistle for confirmation.

"Indeed," Whistle replied. "Sunset is the time when the golden light of day fades, revealing hidden paths and secrets that only the golden ticket can unlock. I'll take you to a place where you can watch the sunset, and together, we'll see where it leads us."

Toby climbed onto the platform, settling into his usual spot, and soon they were chugging down the familiar tracks. As they travelled, the sun began to dip lower in the sky, casting long shadows across the forest. The golden light of dusk bathed the trees, creating a magical glow that made everything feel enchanted.

They reached a clearing on a small hill just as the sun began to set, filling the sky with shades of pink, orange, and gold. Toby held the ticket up to the fading light, hoping for some kind of sign. For a moment, nothing happened, but then he noticed a faint glimmer on the ticket, a small arrow pointing toward a path that led deeper into the forest.

"Look, Whistle! The ticket's showing us the way!" Toby said excitedly.

"Then let's follow it," Whistle replied with a pleased hum. "This is your adventure, Toby. Lead the way."

Toby jumped down from the platform, clutching the ticket as he followed the glowing arrow down the narrow path. Whistle moved slowly along the tracks nearby, keeping pace with him as the path wound deeper into the woods. With each step, the light on the ticket seemed to grow brighter, guiding him forward.

TOBY AND THE TALKING TRAIN 83

After a short while, they came to a hidden clearing Toby had never seen before. In the center of the clearing stood an old wooden gazebo, its roof covered in vines and moss, yet somehow still standing proudly as if it were waiting for him.

The ticket glowed even brighter, and Toby felt a strange pull, as if the gazebo were calling him. He stepped inside, looking around in awe. In the middle of the gazebo lay a small, velvet-covered box, also adorned with golden designs.

Toby reached out, feeling a mix of excitement and nerves as he opened the box. Inside, he found a small compass with a golden needle that sparkled in the fading light. Engraved on the back were the words:

"This compass points not to where you wish to go, but where you need to be."

Toby's eyes widened with wonder. He had never seen a compass like this before, one that pointed to destinations unknown. He felt the weight of the magical object in his hand, sensing that it held a wisdom all its own.

"Whistle, it's a magical compass!" Toby exclaimed, holding it up for his friend to see.

Whistle let out an approving hum. "Yes, and a powerful one at that. This compass will guide you to the places where you're needed most. It's a gift for those who carry kindness in their hearts and curiosity in their minds."

Toby looked down at the compass, feeling a deep sense of responsibility settle over him. "So... it'll take me to places where I can help? Or where I'm meant to learn something?"

"Exactly," Whistle replied. "It's a tool for those who seek purpose beyond themselves. This compass will only guide you when you're ready to listen, and when you're open to what it has to teach."

Toby felt a surge of gratitude, knowing that this was no ordinary adventure. The golden ticket had led him to a gift that would guide him through his life, helping him find the places where he could make a difference.

As the last rays of sunlight faded from the sky, Toby placed the compass carefully back in its box, understanding that it was a treasure to be used with respect. He felt humbled by the journey, realizing that it had brought him closer to understanding his own heart.

"Thank you, Whistle," Toby said, his voice filled with gratitude. "This is the best adventure yet."

Whistle let out a warm, gentle hum, his headlights glowing softly in the evening light. "Remember, Toby, that the compass will always point you in the direction where you're meant to be, but it's up to you to take each step with kindness, courage, and curiosity."

With the compass tucked safely in his pocket, Toby climbed back onto Whistle, feeling as though he had found a new purpose, a calling that went beyond the forest and his own adventures.

As they made their way home under the light of the stars, Toby held the golden compass close, knowing that it would guide him to places and people that needed him, to lessons and mysteries he had yet to discover.

And in his heart, he knew that every journey, every step, would be filled with wonder, as long as he was willing to follow the golden path of purpose that lay before him.

Chapter 20: Through the Mountain

The forest was shrouded in an early morning mist, and the air felt unusually still as Toby arrived at Willow Creek Station. Whistle's headlights cast a warm glow through the fog, and Toby could sense that today's adventure would be something different. He felt a slight flutter of nerves in his stomach, a mixture of excitement and uncertainty.

"Good morning, Toby," Whistle greeted, his voice gentle yet full of purpose.

"Good morning, Whistle," Toby replied, his curiosity piqued by the serious tone in his friend's voice. "What's on the agenda today?"

"I thought we might take a journey through the mountain pass," Whistle said, his headlights flickering thoughtfully. "There's a magical mountain not far from here, and within it lies a path that can help those who seek to face their deepest fears."

Toby's eyes widened. The idea of facing his fears was both thrilling and a bit terrifying. He thought of all the things that frightened him—the dark, heights, being alone—and felt his heart race. But he trusted Whistle and knew that, with his friend by his side, he could be brave.

"I'm ready," he said, taking a deep breath. "Let's do it."

With a low hum of approval, Whistle began to move along the tracks, guiding Toby toward the base of the mountain. The sun rose higher in the sky as they travelled, and soon they reached a hidden trail that wound its way through the dense forest and into the side of a towering, rocky mountain.

The entrance to the mountain was marked by two ancient stone pillars covered in moss and ivy. The tunnel beyond was dark, with only a faint glow emanating from deep within. Toby felt a chill as he looked into the shadows, but he reminded himself that this was a journey of discovery—a chance to face what scared him most.

They entered the tunnel, and the world around them dimmed, the daylight fading until there was only the soft glow from Whistle's headlights to light their way. The walls of the tunnel were lined with strange, sparkling stones that cast faint, shifting colors onto the rocky surface, illuminating the path in an eerie, magical glow.

"Toby," Whistle said, his voice echoing softly in the enclosed space, "this mountain is special. It reveals different things to each person who passes through. It will bring your fears to light, but remember that I'm here with you, every step of the way."

Toby nodded, gripping the edge of the platform as they moved forward. He felt his pulse quicken, but he steadied himself, trusting in Whistle's comforting presence.

They hadn't gone far when the tunnel opened into a large cavern. The walls were covered in beautiful, shimmering crystals, but Toby barely noticed them, for right in the center of the cavern was a dark, narrow bridge that stretched over a deep chasm.

The sight made Toby's heart pound. He had always been afraid of heights, and the bridge looked old and rickety, barely wide enough for a person to cross. Below it was nothing but darkness, the bottom of the chasm hidden from sight.

He hesitated, looking over at Whistle with uncertainty. "I... I don't think I can cross that," he admitted, feeling his palms grow sweaty.

Whistle let out a soft, encouraging hum. "Fear is a powerful feeling, Toby. It often feels larger than it really is. But remember, bravery doesn't mean being without fear—it means moving forward in spite of it."

Toby took a deep breath, repeating Whistle's words in his mind. Gathering his courage, he stepped onto the bridge, gripping the thin rope railing tightly as he took one step, then another. The bridge swayed slightly, and Toby's heart raced, but he kept going, his mind focused on each careful step.

Halfway across, he felt a wave of panic as he looked down, but he took a deep breath, forcing himself to keep his gaze ahead. Step by step, he moved forward until, at last, he reached the other side, where Whistle was waiting, his headlights casting a warm, reassuring glow.

"You did it, Toby," Whistle said, pride evident in his voice.

Toby exhaled, a mixture of relief and pride filling him. He had faced his fear of heights, and even though his legs were shaky, he felt stronger for having crossed the bridge.

They continued deeper into the mountain, winding through narrow tunnels and past glittering stone formations. But soon, they entered another cavern, and this one was completely dark. Toby could barely see a few feet ahead, even with Whistle's headlights illuminating the space.

A sense of dread settled over him. He had always been afraid of the dark, of the unknown that lay within it. The cavern seemed to press in around him, making his skin prickle with fear.

"Toby," Whistle said gently, sensing his discomfort, "sometimes, when we face darkness, we realize that it isn't as frightening as it seems. Let's stay still for a moment, and let your eyes adjust."

Toby nodded, taking a deep breath as he stood beside Whistle, his hands gripping the platform. He closed his eyes, then opened them, allowing himself to feel the darkness without trying to resist it. Slowly, he noticed small, glowing dots appearing on the walls around him—tiny, bioluminescent fungi that began to light up like stars.

The cavern transformed, the soft glow of the fungi creating a beautiful, otherworldly effect. Toby's fear began to fade as he took in the sight, realizing that even the darkness could hold beauty and wonder if he allowed himself to see it.

"Thank you, Whistle," Toby said, his voice soft with awe. "I would have missed all of this if I hadn't faced my fear."

"You see, Toby," Whistle replied, "fear is often a veil that hides something beautiful. When we confront it, we learn that we are braver and stronger than we ever realized."

Feeling empowered, Toby followed Whistle as they made their way out of the dark cavern and into the final stretch of the tunnel. Just as they neared the exit, Toby felt a pang of sadness—his last fear, the fear of being alone. He worried that someday, his adventures with Whistle might end, or that he'd be left without his friend.

But as they reached the mouth of the tunnel, Toby felt Whistle's familiar, reassuring hum.

"Toby," Whistle said, his voice filled with warmth, "you are never truly alone. You carry the memories of those you love, the strength of the lessons you've learned, and the magic of our friendship within you. Those things will always be with you."

A deep sense of comfort filled Toby's heart. He realized that his bond with Whistle, and with all his friends in the forest, was something that could never be lost. It was a part of him now, a source of strength he could carry wherever he went.

As they emerged from the mountain, the morning sunlight spilled over the landscape, bathing the forest in a golden glow. Toby took a deep breath, feeling a new sense of confidence and peace. He had faced his fears, each one revealing a strength he hadn't known he had.

"Thank you, Whistle," Toby said, looking up at his friend with gratitude. "I feel... different. Stronger."

Whistle gave a gentle, approving hum. "You are, Toby. Every fear you face teaches you more about yourself. Bravery isn't about having no fears; it's about choosing to confront them and learning from them."

As Toby made his way home, he felt a renewed sense of courage, knowing that he could face any challenge that came his way. The mountain had shown him that his fears, while powerful, were conquerable, and that his strength came from within.

And with Whistle by his side, he knew he would never be truly alone, no matter what adventures awaited him.

Chapter 21: Meeting the Train Family

It was a bright, crisp morning, and the forest seemed to hum with excitement as Toby made his way to Willow Creek Station. He had no idea what today's adventure would bring, but his heart felt light and eager. When he reached the station, Whistle greeted him with an extra cheerful hum, as if he were holding back a wonderful surprise.

"Good morning, Whistle!" Toby called, sensing that today was no ordinary day.

"Good morning, Toby," Whistle replied, his voice full of warmth. "Today, I thought it was time to introduce you to some very special friends—my family."

Toby's eyes widened with excitement. "Your family? There are more magical trains like you?"

Whistle let out a soft chuckle. "Yes, Toby. Magical trains have a way of finding each other. We may be hidden from most of the world, but we share a bond, and each of us has a unique role in helping others. Today, I'd like you to meet a few of them."

With a thrill of anticipation, Toby climbed onto Whistle's platform, eager to meet the magical trains that Whistle called family. They set off along a winding track that led deep into the forest, through tunnels of trees and over bridges covered in moss. As they travelled, Toby felt a growing sense of wonder. He had always known that Whistle was special, but the thought of meeting other magical trains filled him with awe.

After a short journey, they arrived at a hidden clearing with tracks that branched off in every direction. There, gathered in the dappled sunlight, were three other trains, each distinct and beautiful in their own way.

The first train was sleek and silver, with a shimmering finish that reflected the sunlight like a river. Her headlights shone with a soft blue light, and her voice was gentle and soothing.

"This is Luna," Whistle introduced. "She's known as the Dreamkeeper. Luna travels at night, bringing peaceful dreams to those who need rest and calm. She has a gift for understanding people's hearts, helping them find comfort while they sleep."

Toby stepped closer, gazing at Luna in wonder. "Hello, Luna. It's so nice to meet you."

Luna let out a soft, melodic hum. "Hello, Toby. I've heard much about you. It's a pleasure to finally meet the young Listener who has brought so much joy to Whistle."

Toby smiled, feeling a gentle warmth from Luna. He could sense the calming energy she radiated, and he imagined her gliding through the night, bringing dreams to those who needed a touch of peace.

Next to Luna was a sturdy train with a deep green color, covered in vines and tiny wildflowers that seemed to have grown right into his frame. His headlights were warm and earthy, and he had a deep, reassuring voice.

"This is Evergreen," Whistle said, introducing the train with a nod of respect. "He is the Guardian of the Forest. Evergreen travels through woods and valleys, protecting the animals, plants, and natural wonders of the forest. He keeps the balance, making sure that nature and magic remain in harmony."

Toby's eyes sparkled as he greeted Evergreen. "Hello, Evergreen. Thank you for taking care of the forest. It's one of my favourite places."

Evergreen gave a hearty chuckle, his voice deep like the roots of a great tree. "It's good to meet a friend of the forest, Toby. Whistle tells me you have a kind heart, and I can see why he chose you as his Listener."

Toby felt a sense of awe and gratitude as he looked at Evergreen. He thought of all the animals and plants that thrived in the forest, realizing that Evergreen had a hand in preserving their beauty and balance.

The last train was bright and colorful, painted in shades of red, orange, and yellow, as if he were carrying a bit of the sunset with him.

His voice was lively and warm, filled with a contagious energy that made Toby smile instantly.

"And this," Whistle said, his voice filled with affection, "is Spark. He's the Bringer of Joy. Spark travels to towns and villages, spreading cheer with his music, lights, and laughter. He lifts people's spirits wherever he goes."

Toby laughed, feeling the warmth radiate from Spark as he greeted him. "Hi, Spark! I bet you're really fun to be around."

Spark let out a joyful honk, his headlights twinkling with amusement. "That's right, Toby! Life is meant to be enjoyed, and I do my best to make sure everyone remembers to have a little fun along the way."

Toby couldn't help but laugh along with Spark. Each of these trains, he realized, had a unique role, a special purpose that helped make the world a better place. They were all different, yet connected by the same spirit of kindness and magic.

After the introductions, Whistle spoke again. "Each of us has our own path, our own way of helping others. And while we may not always travel together, we're connected by the magic of our purpose."

Toby looked around at the trains, feeling a deep sense of appreciation for each one of them. "It's amazing," he said, his voice filled with wonder. "You're all like a family, helping people in ways that are unique to you. And even though I only see Whistle most of the time, it feels like I know you all, too."

Luna nodded, her voice soft and wise. "Family isn't just about being together, Toby. It's about supporting each other, even from afar, and knowing that we're all part of something greater than ourselves."

Evergreen added, "We may travel different paths, but we all share the same goal: to help and protect, to bring light and balance into the world."

Spark chimed in with a cheerful honk. "And a little joy never hurt, either!"

Toby laughed, feeling a warmth fill his heart as he stood among the trains. He understood now that Whistle was part of a bigger purpose, a network of magical trains each with their own mission. And in a way, Toby felt like he was part of that mission, too—a Listener who could help carry on the magic of their work.

"Thank you for letting me meet your family, Whistle," Toby said, his voice full of gratitude. "I feel lucky to know each of you. I promise to do my part to help, even in small ways."

Whistle gave a gentle, approving hum. "You're already part of our family, Toby. Your kindness, curiosity, and bravery have shown that you belong with us. And as long as you carry our lessons with you, you'll be helping us in ways you can't even imagine."

As the sun began to set, casting a warm glow over the clearing, the other trains began to prepare for their journeys. Luna gave Toby a gentle nod, Evergreen let out a deep, earthy hum of gratitude, and Spark honked cheerfully before setting off in a flash of color.

Toby watched them go, feeling a sense of connection and belonging he hadn't felt before. Meeting Whistle's family had shown him that there were many ways to make a difference in the world, and that each person—or train—could contribute something unique.

As Whistle began the journey back to Willow Creek Station, Toby looked up at his friend with a smile. "I think I understand now, Whistle. Even though I'm just one person, I can make a difference, too. Just like you and your family."

Whistle let out a gentle hum. "That's right, Toby. Each of us has a role to play, and together, we create a world filled with kindness, wonder, and magic. And your role, Toby, is just as important."

Toby felt a deep sense of purpose settle within him. He knew that his adventures with Whistle were part of something much bigger, and that, in his own way, he was helping to carry on the magic of the train family's mission.

As they travelled through the twilight, Toby felt a quiet joy in his heart, knowing that he was part of a magical family—a family that believed in the power of kindness, joy, and wisdom to light up the world. And with Whistle by his side, he was ready to carry that light wherever he went.

Chapter 22: The Day of Distractions

It was a bright, busy Saturday morning, and Toby was full of energy as he made his way through the forest toward Willow Creek Station. Today was special because he had promised to help Whistle with a long-overdue cleaning and maintenance day. Toby knew it was important to keep Whistle in top shape, especially with all the magical journeys they went on. He was determined to make sure his friend was polished, checked, and ready for any adventure.

As he neared the clearing, Toby was already thinking about everything he needed to do: clean Whistle's headlights, polish the panels, and check the gears and wheels. He wanted to make sure Whistle felt as good as new.

"Good morning, Whistle!" Toby greeted, his voice full of enthusiasm.

"Good morning, Toby," Whistle replied warmly. "Thank you for coming to help today. I appreciate your care and attention."

"Of course!" Toby said, feeling a sense of pride and purpose. "Let's get started!"

But just as Toby was about to begin, he heard a familiar bark. He turned around and saw his neighbour's dog, Max, bounding through the trees. Max ran up to Toby, tail wagging and eyes bright, dropping a stick at his feet as if inviting him to play.

Toby hesitated. Max was a fun playmate, always full of energy, and Toby felt a pull to join him. But he quickly remembered his promise to Whistle and shook his head. "Not now, Max. I'm here to help Whistle today."

Max barked again, nudging the stick closer, his eyes hopeful. Toby felt another twinge of temptation. "Just one throw," he reasoned, picking up the stick and tossing it a short distance. Max dashed after it, and Toby laughed as he watched the dog's excitement.

But soon, one throw turned into two, then three, and before he knew it, ten minutes had gone by. Toby glanced back at Whistle, who was waiting patiently. He felt a pang of guilt and called out, "I'm coming, Whistle! I got a bit distracted, but I'm ready to start now."

With renewed focus, Toby grabbed a soft cloth from his backpack and began polishing Whistle's panels. The smooth, rhythmic motion helped him focus, and he began to feel a sense of calm as he worked. But just as he was getting into a steady rhythm, he heard a shout from the path.

"Toby!" his friend Leo called, riding up on his bicycle. "Come check out my new bike! It's got these awesome new gears and a bell!"

Toby looked over, excitement flaring up. Leo's bike was sleek and bright, with shiny new gears and a flashing red light on the back. Toby was instantly fascinated, wanting to know all about it.

For a moment, he felt torn. Helping Whistle was important, but so was spending time with Leo and seeing his friend's new bike. "It won't take long to look," Toby told himself, putting the cloth down. "Just a quick peek."

He walked over to Leo, admiring the bike and asking questions about the new features. They chatted and laughed, talking about how fast the bike could go and planning a bike race for another day. But as the minutes passed, Toby remembered Whistle waiting for him and felt a pang of guilt.

"I'd better get back," Toby told Leo reluctantly. "I promised Whistle I'd help him today."

Leo nodded, understanding. "Alright, see you later, Toby!"

Returning to Whistle, Toby felt frustrated with himself. He had been distracted twice now, even though he'd come with the intention to stay focused. He picked up the cloth again, determined to finish polishing Whistle's panels without any more interruptions.

But as he started back on his task, he heard a rustling in the bushes nearby. Out of the corner of his eye, he saw Finn, the clever fox, trotting toward him with his usual mischievous grin.

"Hello, Toby!" Finn greeted, his eyes sparkling with curiosity. "There's a family of hedgehogs down by the creek. Want to come see? They're just waking up for the day, and they're quite a sight!"

Toby bit his lip, feeling torn yet again. He loved watching the animals in the forest, and seeing a family of hedgehogs would be amazing. But he knew that if he went, he'd lose even more time.

"I... I really want to, Finn," Toby said, struggling with the decision. "But I promised Whistle I'd help him today, and I've already gotten distracted a couple of times."

Finn nodded, his gaze thoughtful. "I understand, Toby. Keeping promises is important, especially when someone's counting on you. Perhaps the hedgehogs will still be there later."

Toby smiled gratefully. "Thanks, Finn. I'll come find you once I'm done helping Whistle."

With a sense of relief, Toby returned to Whistle and focused on his task with renewed determination. As he carefully polished Whistle's panels, he began to understand the importance of sticking to a promise, especially when it was difficult to stay focused. He realized that each distraction, though tempting, was pulling him away from something he had committed to—and that it took real effort and perseverance to keep his word.

Finally, after what felt like a long and careful effort, Toby finished polishing Whistle's panels. He stepped back, admiring the clean, gleaming surface, and felt a deep sense of accomplishment. Whistle looked brighter and fresher, and Toby knew that he had done his part to care for his friend.

"Thank you, Toby," Whistle said, his voice full of appreciation. "Your dedication means a lot to me. I know it wasn't easy with so many things calling your attention."

Toby felt a swell of pride. "I'm sorry I got distracted, Whistle. I didn't realize how hard it would be to stay focused. But I learned that keeping a promise means sticking to it, even when there are other things I'd like to do."

Whistle let out a soft, approving hum. "That's the essence of perseverance, Toby. It's easy to be committed when things are simple, but true dedication shines through when you choose to stay focused despite distractions. You've shown that you can stay the course, and that makes your promise even more meaningful."

Toby nodded, feeling the weight of Whistle's words. He realized that perseverance wasn't just about finishing a task—it was about honouring his word and showing that he valued his commitments. With this new understanding, he felt a renewed sense of responsibility and strength.

As the sun began to set, Toby took a moment to look around, feeling grateful for the lesson he had learned. He knew there would always be distractions, things that would tempt him away from his commitments, but he felt more prepared to face them.

Before he left, Finn returned, a mischievous smile on his face. "Good job, Toby. The hedgehogs are still there, by the way. Ready to see them now?"

Toby grinned, feeling a deep sense of satisfaction. "Yes, Finn, I'd love to."

With Whistle's hum of approval echoing behind him, Toby followed Finn down to the creek, feeling the strength of his own perseverance carry him forward. He knew now that every promise he made was a choice, a commitment, and with a bit of focus and effort, he could keep it—no matter what distractions lay in his path.

Chapter 23: The Hidden Valley of Wishes

It was a breezy autumn afternoon when Toby arrived at Willow Creek Station, ready for another adventure with Whistle. The leaves were a patchwork of reds, yellows, and oranges, and the forest seemed to whisper secrets as they rustled in the wind. Toby felt a surge of excitement, wondering where Whistle might take him today.

As soon as he climbed onto the platform, Whistle let out a soft hum of anticipation. "Good afternoon, Toby. Today, I thought we might visit a very special place—one hidden deep within the forest, known only to those who are meant to find it."

Toby's eyes sparkled with curiosity. "Where are we going, Whistle?"

Whistle's headlights flickered as he replied, "To the Hidden Valley of Wishes. It's a magical place, where wishes come true. But be warned, Toby: wishes hold a powerful magic, and once made, they cannot be undone. Today, you'll learn the importance of thinking carefully before wishing."

Toby felt a thrill of excitement mixed with a tinge of nervousness. Wishes that come true? He'd never heard of such a place. But the idea of visiting a valley where anything he wanted might happen filled him with wonder.

"I'm ready," he said, filled with anticipation.

With a hum of approval, Whistle set off, winding along unfamiliar tracks that twisted and turned deeper into the forest than they had ever gone before. The trees grew taller, and the sunlight filtered through in dappled patterns, casting a gentle, mysterious glow. After a while, they reached a secluded pathway that led into a hidden valley surrounded by tall hills.

As they entered the valley, Toby felt a shift in the air. The valley was bathed in a golden light, even though it was still afternoon. Everything glowed softly—the trees, the grass, and even the rocks seemed to sparkle. It felt like stepping into a dream.

In the center of the valley stood a small, ancient stone well. Beside it was a sign, beautifully carved, that read: "The Well of Wishes. Speak wisely, for your words hold power."

Toby approached the well, his heart pounding with excitement. He had always dreamed about making wishes, imagining all the wonderful things he could ask for. But as he stood there, looking down into the still, clear water, he began to feel the weight of Whistle's words: Think carefully before you wish.

"Toby," Whistle said gently, "the valley grants wishes that come from the heart. But remember, wishes are like seeds—once planted, they grow in ways we cannot always control. Make sure that what you wish for is something you truly want."

Toby nodded, gazing into the well as he thought. His mind raced with ideas, each wish seeming more exciting than the last. He could wish for a never-ending adventure, or perhaps for more magical places to explore. But he hesitated, feeling the importance of making the right choice.

Just then, he heard a soft, distant voice calling his name. He turned, surprised, and saw a flicker of movement by the edge of the valley. He walked over and found a small, shimmering creature—a forest sprite, with wings like leaves and a tiny, glowing lantern in her hand.

"Hello, Toby," the sprite said in a soft, tinkling voice. "I am Lyra, a guardian of the valley. I watch over the wishes made here and help those who seek guidance."

"Hello, Lyra," Toby replied, captivated by her presence. "I... I'm not sure what to wish for. There are so many things I want, but I don't know which one is right."

Lyra smiled, her wings fluttering softly. "That is the challenge of a wish. Many come here with grand desires, wishing for wealth or fame, only to find that these wishes don't bring the happiness they imagined. True wishes come from the heart, Toby. They bring joy not only to the wisher but to those around them as well."

Toby thought about this, realizing that a wish was more than just getting something he wanted. He wanted his wish to mean something, to bring good not just to him, but perhaps to Whistle, the forest, and all his friends.

He looked back at the well, then at Lyra, and finally at Whistle. A thought began to form in his mind—a wish that he felt truly mattered.

Taking a deep breath, Toby leaned over the well and spoke softly, "I wish for my heart to always be brave, kind, and open to learning, so I can be a good friend to everyone around me."

As his words echoed in the stillness, the valley seemed to come alive. A gentle breeze swept through, and the golden light grew brighter, as if the valley itself approved of his wish. The well shimmered, and a tiny golden spark rose from the water, drifting up into the sky before disappearing like a star.

Lyra smiled warmly, her eyes shining with approval. "A wise and selfless wish, Toby. You have chosen well. Such a wish will grow within you, helping you face all the challenges and joys that come your way."

Toby felt a warmth settle in his chest, a sense of peace and purpose that filled him from within. He knew that his wish would be a lifelong journey, one that would shape who he was and who he would become. It was a wish that would guide him, much like Whistle, through all of life's adventures.

As they prepared to leave the valley, Whistle let out a gentle, proud hum. "Toby, you've shown that you truly understand the power of a wish. You chose not just for yourself, but for those around you. That is the mark of a true Listener, one who brings kindness and thoughtfulness into the world."

Toby smiled, feeling the weight of his wish settle in a comforting way. He knew he could have wished for something grand or exciting, but he was grateful for the reminder that sometimes, the simplest wishes held the greatest power.

As they made their way out of the valley, Toby glanced back one last time. The golden light of the valley faded gently, returning to the soft hues of the forest, as if the valley itself had gone back to sleep, awaiting the next visitor.

On the journey home, Toby felt a quiet strength within him, knowing that he had made a wish he could carry with him always. It was a wish that would help him face any challenge, and one that would remind him of the importance of kindness, bravery, and learning.

And with Whistle by his side, Toby knew that every day would bring new opportunities to grow, to learn, and to make the world a little brighter—one thoughtful wish at a time.

Chapter 24: The Missing Ticket Puzzle

It was an unusually windy morning when Toby arrived at Willow Creek Station. The gusts of wind rustled through the trees, scattering leaves across the tracks. As Toby approached, he noticed Whistle waiting with a sense of urgency.

"Toby!" Whistle called out as soon as he saw him. "I need your help with a bit of a mystery today."

Toby's curiosity piqued immediately. "What's going on, Whistle?"

"It appears that someone left behind a special train ticket," Whistle explained, "but it's no ordinary ticket. This one has the power to transport its holder to any magical destination they wish. Without it, they'll miss their journey and the opportunity to discover something extraordinary."

Toby's eyes widened. A magical ticket that could take someone anywhere they desired? He couldn't imagine anything more exciting! "Where is it? Do you know who it belongs to?"

Whistle gave a thoughtful hum. "The ticket was last seen right here at the station, but now it's gone. I believe it's hidden somewhere close by, and we'll need to follow a series of clues to find it. It's as though the ticket wants to be found only by someone clever enough to solve its puzzle."

Toby's heart leapt with excitement. Solving a puzzle to uncover a magical ticket sounded like the perfect adventure. "I'm ready, Whistle! Let's find that ticket!"

Whistle let out a soft chuckle. "Excellent, Toby. Here's the first clue." From a compartment, Whistle produced a small slip of paper with a riddle written on it in elegant script:

"To start your journey, look beneath the stone,
Where moss and ivy have gently grown.
There lies a clue to the path ahead,
Beneath the green and leafy bed."

Toby read the clue aloud, then looked around the station, spotting a large stone near the edge of the platform covered in soft moss and strands of ivy. "I think I know where to start!" he exclaimed.

He crouched beside the stone, carefully brushing aside the ivy and moss. Beneath it, he found a small wooden box. Inside was a slip of paper with the next clue:

"Where water flows and small fish play,
Look for the rocks stacked in a curious way.
There lies your next step in the quest,
Hidden by nature, as it's been blessed."

Toby grinned, knowing exactly where to go. There was a small stream just beyond the station, where he'd often seen minnows darting around the rocks. He ran to the stream, scanning the area until he spotted a few rocks stacked in a neat little tower, almost like a marker.

As he approached, he noticed something tucked beneath the base of the rock stack—a piece of folded parchment. Opening it, he read the next clue:

"The roots of wisdom grow strong and deep,
By an old oak where squirrels leap.
In a hollow hidden from sight,
You'll find the answer to set things right."

Toby thought for a moment, recalling an ancient oak tree near the path that led to Willow Creek Station. The tree was large and weathered, with thick roots and a hollowed-out nook at its base. He'd seen squirrels darting around it often.

He jogged over to the oak tree, feeling the thrill of the hunt, and carefully reached into the hollow. His fingers brushed against something smooth and cold. He pulled it out—a small metal tin with another slip of paper inside.

Unfolding it, he read the final clue:
"To solve the puzzle and find the prize,
Look where Whistle shines bright with wise eyes.

Near the light that guides the way,
You'll find what's lost, come what may."

Toby's eyes lit up as he realized the answer. Whistle's headlights! The ticket must be near Whistle's headlights, the "wise eyes" that always guided their way.

He hurried back to Whistle, excitement bubbling within him. Standing beside Whistle, he scanned the area near the headlights and noticed a small glint beneath one of the headlamps. Reaching in carefully, he pulled out a small, golden ticket with intricate designs etched along its edges.

"We found it, Whistle! The missing ticket!" Toby said, holding it up triumphantly.

Whistle let out a joyful whistle. "Well done, Toby! You solved each clue with patience and cleverness. This ticket will now return to its rightful owner, and you've proven yourself as a true problem-solver."

Toby smiled, feeling a sense of pride. Solving the puzzle had been thrilling, but it also taught him the importance of staying focused and thinking carefully. He realized that each step had required him to pay attention to details and think creatively, and he'd enjoyed every moment of the challenge.

"Thank you, Whistle. That was the best puzzle I've ever solved," Toby said, still clutching the golden ticket.

Whistle let out a warm hum. "Remember, Toby, that solving a problem isn't just about finding the answer—it's about the journey you take to get there. And you showed true perseverance today."

As the sun began to set, Toby looked at the ticket one last time before handing it to Whistle, knowing that it would soon find its way back to its owner. He felt a deep sense of accomplishment, grateful for the lesson and the adventure.

With the puzzle solved and the ticket safe, Toby headed home, his heart full of excitement and satisfaction. He knew that, thanks to

Whistle, he'd honed his problem-solving skills—and that any future puzzle or challenge would be an opportunity for discovery and growth.

Chapter 25: The Tale of the First Talking Train

The forest was calm and quiet, wrapped in the soft glow of the setting sun, as Toby arrived at Willow Creek Station. He loved these moments with Whistle—the gentle stillness of the twilight and the way the air seemed filled with possibilities.

Today, though, Whistle looked particularly thoughtful, as if he were holding onto a story he was ready to share. His headlights glowed softly as Toby approached, and he greeted Toby with a warm, gentle hum.

"Hello, Whistle," Toby said, sensing something special in the air. "Is everything alright?"

Whistle let out a soft, almost wistful hum. "Yes, Toby, everything is quite alright. But tonight, I'd like to tell you a story—a story from long, long ago, about the very first talking train."

Toby's eyes lit up with excitement. He had always wondered how the magic of talking trains began, and he felt honoured that Whistle was willing to share such an important story with him. "I'd love to hear it," he said, settling down beside Whistle.

With a deep, steady hum, Whistle began.

"A long, long time ago, before most people even knew about magical trains, there was a small, unassuming train named Aurora. She was built like any other train—strong and steady, with a sturdy engine and wheels meant to carry people and cargo across vast distances. But Aurora had something unique, something no other train possessed: a voice."

Toby listened intently, imagining the small, mysterious train traveling alone, filled with a magic that no one else knew about.

"At first, Aurora kept her voice a secret," Whistle continued. "She feared that people might not understand, that they'd be frightened of her uniqueness. After all, no one had ever heard a train speak before. So she travelled quietly, carrying people and goods, watching over those around her with a silent kindness."

Whistle paused, as if lost in the memory of those ancient days. "But one night, during a terrible storm, Aurora heard the frightened cries of a young child who had become separated from his family. The child had wandered onto the tracks, alone and scared, as the storm raged around him."

Toby's heart raced as he imagined the scene—the pouring rain, the wind howling through the trees, and the frightened child huddled on the tracks.

"Aurora knew that if she stayed silent, the child would remain lost, vulnerable to the dangers of the storm. In that moment, she realized that her voice was not something to hide—it was a gift, something that could help others. She gently called out to the child, guiding him with her voice, comforting him and keeping him safe until his family found him."

Toby felt a surge of admiration for Aurora. "She used her voice to help others, even though it was risky?"

"Exactly," Whistle replied, his voice filled with warmth. "Aurora discovered that her uniqueness, her voice, could bring comfort and safety to others. From that day forward, she never hid her gift again. She became known as the First Talking Train, traveling far and wide, helping people, guiding them, and even telling stories to soothe weary travellers on long journeys."

Toby thought about this, letting the story sink in. "So... was she the only one?"

Whistle let out a gentle chuckle. "No, Toby. Over time, other trains found their voices, each discovering the magic within themselves in different ways. Some could talk like Aurora, while others could communicate through whistles or hums, sharing their wisdom in quieter ways. And just like people, each train found its own unique way of helping the world."

Toby felt a deep sense of connection to Aurora's story. "I think I understand now. It's not just about being magical or different—it's about using what makes us unique to help others."

Whistle hummed in approval. "That's right, Toby. Aurora's tale reminds us that our differences are gifts, and that each of us has something special to offer. Even if the world doesn't always understand, embracing who we are allows us to make a difference."

Toby looked at Whistle, his heart filled with gratitude. He thought about the moments when he'd felt different, times when he'd been unsure of himself. Aurora's story reminded him that uniqueness was something to be celebrated, not hidden.

"Thank you, Whistle," Toby said, his voice quiet but full of emotion. "Sometimes, I wonder if being different makes me strange, but... now I see it makes me special, too. Just like Aurora."

Whistle gave a soft, approving hum. "Remember, Toby, that every gift—no matter how unusual—has a purpose. When we embrace who we are, we not only help ourselves but can bring light and joy to others. Aurora's voice was a beacon, and so is yours."

The two sat in comfortable silence, the night settling gently over the forest. Toby looked up at the stars, feeling as if Aurora's spirit was there, watching over them. He thought about all the people, and even trains, who might feel out of place, and he wished they could hear Aurora's story.

As Toby prepared to leave for the night, he turned to Whistle, his heart brimming with gratitude. "I promise, Whistle, that I'll remember Aurora's story, and I'll try my best to use my own gifts to help others, just like she did."

Whistle let out a contented hum, his headlights glowing softly. "I have no doubt you will, Toby. You already have. And remember, every journey you take, every lesson you learn, brings you closer to discovering more of who you are."

With a final look at Whistle, Toby made his way home, the tale of the First Talking Train filling him with warmth and inspiration. He knew that no matter where life took him, he would carry Aurora's legacy with him, using his own unique gifts to make the world a little brighter.

As he walked through the forest, he felt more certain than ever that being different was a strength, a kind of magic all its own. And with Whistle and Aurora's story to guide him, he was ready to embrace every part of himself, knowing that his own voice—just like Aurora's—had the power to make a difference.

Chapter 26: An Unexpected Detour

It was a clear, chilly morning, and Toby was in high spirits as he arrived at Willow Creek Station. He and Whistle had planned an exciting journey to explore a new part of the forest they'd never seen before. Toby had packed a small backpack with snacks and his notebook, ready to record any discoveries they might come across.

"Good morning, Whistle! I'm ready for our adventure!" Toby called, climbing up onto the platform.

"Good morning, Toby," Whistle replied, his headlights flickering with anticipation. "We have a beautiful route ahead of us, filled with new sights and trails. Let's set off!"

With a cheerful hum, Whistle began moving along the tracks, and they soon found themselves winding through a dense part of the forest, filled with towering trees and thick patches of ferns. The early morning sunlight filtered through the branches, casting soft shadows that made everything look magical.

As they travelled deeper into the woods, a faint sound reached Toby's ears. At first, he thought it might be the wind, but as they moved closer, he realized it was something different—a soft, distressed chirping, almost like a call for help.

"Did you hear that, Whistle?" Toby asked, turning his head toward the sound.

Whistle slowed down, his headlights flickering thoughtfully. "Yes, Toby. It sounds like a creature in need. Perhaps we should take a look?"

Toby nodded, his sense of adventure quickly shifting to a feeling of concern. "Yes, let's check it out. Maybe we can help."

Following the sound, Whistle veered slightly off their intended route, making a gentle detour along a narrower path. As they approached a clearing, Toby spotted a small bird huddled at the base of a tree, its feathers ruffled and one wing held awkwardly. The bird looked frightened and hurt, chirping softly as it tried to move.

Toby climbed down from the platform and approached the bird slowly, speaking in a calm, soothing voice. "Hey there, little one. It's okay. We're here to help."

The bird looked up at him with wide, anxious eyes, but it didn't try to fly away, as if it understood that Toby meant no harm. Toby knelt beside it, gently examining its wing. "It looks like it might be sprained," he said, glancing back at Whistle. "It can't fly like this."

Whistle hummed thoughtfully, his headlights focused on the small creature. "Sometimes, our journey takes us to unexpected places, Toby. Helping others, especially those who cannot help themselves, is a path worth taking."

Toby nodded, feeling a warmth in his heart as he realized this adventure was turning out to be something different than he had expected. "You're right, Whistle. Let's take care of our little friend."

Carefully, Toby fashioned a small nest out of the soft leaves and moss nearby, creating a gentle bed for the bird to rest in. He sat beside it, speaking softly to keep it calm, while Whistle offered his warm headlights to create a comforting glow.

"I'll stay with you," Toby said to the bird, who chirped softly, as if in thanks.

The three of them stayed together in the clearing, the quiet sounds of the forest surrounding them. Toby realized that this moment—sitting quietly, helping the injured bird—was as meaningful as any adventure he could have imagined. He thought about how easy it would have been to ignore the small chirps and keep moving, but he knew now that listening and helping were as much a part of the journey as reaching a destination.

After a while, the bird's breathing seemed to slow, and it appeared more relaxed, settling into the makeshift nest as though it felt safe in their presence.

"I think our friend feels a little better," Toby said, smiling. "Maybe it just needed a bit of warmth and company."

"Sometimes, all it takes is a bit of kindness and patience," Whistle replied gently. "Every life, no matter how small, deserves care and attention."

As they waited, a soft rustling came from the nearby bushes. Toby looked up, spotting another bird, similar in color and markings, hopping toward them. It chirped softly, its eyes fixed on the injured bird in the nest, and Toby realized it must be a family member—a partner or a friend, coming to check on its loved one.

The injured bird chirped back, a hopeful sound that filled the clearing with a sense of relief and happiness. Toby carefully stepped back, giving the birds space as they reunited. The two birds shared a gentle moment together, their soft chirps filled with comfort and reassurance.

Toby watched the scene, feeling a deep sense of joy. He knew now that this unexpected detour had been worth every moment.

"Thank you, Whistle," Toby said, looking up at his friend with gratitude. "For reminding me that helping others is sometimes the best adventure."

Whistle let out a gentle, proud hum. "Kindness is a gift, Toby. Sometimes, the greatest journeys are those where we stop and lend a hand, making the world a little brighter for someone in need."

As they watched the two birds together, the uninjured bird gently nudged the injured one, as if encouraging it. With a tentative flutter, the injured bird spread its wings, testing its strength. Slowly but surely, it managed to lift itself a few inches off the ground, landing softly beside its friend. Toby and Whistle held their breath, watching with hope and excitement as the injured bird tried again, gaining a bit more height this time.

After a few more attempts, the injured bird took off into the air, flying alongside its companion as they disappeared into the trees together.

Toby felt a rush of happiness, his heart filled with a sense of accomplishment. He looked at Whistle with a broad smile. "We did it! Our little friend is back with its family."

Whistle gave a soft, contented hum, his headlights glowing warmly. "And so, our unexpected journey comes to a joyful end. Sometimes, the best paths are the ones we don't plan, and the greatest gifts are those we give without expecting anything in return."

Toby nodded, feeling a newfound understanding of what it meant to help others. He realized that every choice, even a small one like stopping to help a bird, could make a big difference. He knew now that kindness was a journey in itself—one that could bring unexpected joy and meaning.

As they returned to their original path, Toby felt a deeper appreciation for the journey he was on, and for Whistle, who had taught him so much about compassion and patience. He knew that he'd carry this lesson with him always, reminding himself to listen, to care, and to help those in need—no matter where the road might take him.

With a final look at the spot where the birds had flown away, Toby climbed back onto Whistle with a heart full of gratitude. They continued down the tracks, the forest alive with a newfound glow, as if it, too, celebrated their small act of kindness. And with Whistle by his side, Toby was ready for whatever detours life had in store, knowing that every path could lead to a meaningful adventure.

Chapter 27: The Enchanted Forest

The forest was bathed in a soft, mysterious light as Toby arrived at Willow Creek Station. The air felt different that morning, as if something magical lingered in every shadow and beam of sunlight. He could sense the promise of an extraordinary adventure, and Whistle seemed to share his excitement, his headlights glowing brighter than usual.

"Good morning, Whistle," Toby said, his voice filled with anticipation. "Is there something special planned for today?"

Whistle let out a gentle, knowing hum. "Indeed, Toby. Today, we'll be exploring a part of the forest that few have ever seen—a place known as the Enchanted Forest. This is a place where nature's magic is especially strong, and where the creatures have wisdom and secrets to share with those who listen."

Toby's eyes lit up with wonder. He had heard tales of enchanted forests, places filled with magical creatures and hidden mysteries, but he had never imagined he'd be able to see one himself. "That sounds amazing! I'll be sure to listen carefully."

With a hum of approval, Whistle began moving along the tracks, guiding them through the familiar woods until they reached a path he had never noticed before. The trees grew denser, their branches intertwining overhead to form a canopy that cast dappled shadows on the ground. The air grew cooler, filled with the scent of earth and flowers, and tiny glimmers of light sparkled here and there, like stars among the leaves.

As they ventured deeper, Toby noticed unusual plants along the path—flowers that glowed faintly, vines that twisted in beautiful patterns, and mushrooms that shimmered in soft pastel hues. Everything seemed alive, humming with a quiet, magical energy.

After a short journey, they arrived in a wide clearing, where a group of creatures awaited them. Toby's breath caught in awe. Standing among the trees were beings he had only read about—graceful deer with antlers woven with flowers, tiny, winged sprites that flitted about like butterflies, and even a wise-looking tortoise with stones glinting on its shell.

One of the deer, tall and regal, stepped forward. Her antlers held a crown of blossoms, and her gentle eyes were filled with kindness and wisdom. "Welcome, Toby and Whistle. We are the guardians of this forest, and it is an honour to meet a young Listener who respects the ways of nature."

Toby bowed slightly, feeling both humbled and grateful. "Thank you for welcoming us. I'm here to learn whatever you're willing to share."

The deer nodded, her gaze warm. "The Enchanted Forest is a place of balance, where every plant and creature lives in harmony. But to keep this balance, it is essential that all who visit understand the importance of respecting nature."

As she spoke, a small sprite with glittering wings flew up to Toby, her eyes bright with curiosity. "Do you know why the plants and animals here thrive so beautifully?" she asked in a voice as soft as a whispering breeze.

Toby shook his head, eager to learn.

"Because we care for each other," the sprite continued. "Every creature plays a role. The trees provide shelter for the animals, the flowers feed the bees, and even the smallest insects help the plants grow. We're all connected."

Toby looked around, realizing that every plant, animal, and magical creature in the forest depended on each other to thrive. It reminded him of his own friends and family, how they looked out for each other and helped each other grow.

A fox with silvery fur approached, his eyes sharp and wise. "Respecting nature means understanding that every action has a consequence. When we take something from the forest, we give something back. When we walk here, we tread lightly. Nature is a gift, and it must be cherished."

Toby nodded, taking in the fox's words. He thought about how, in his everyday life, he could make choices that were kind to nature—being careful not to waste, picking up litter, and appreciating the world around him.

Just then, the wise tortoise with stones on his shell spoke up, his voice deep and slow. "Patience, young one, is also a part of respecting nature. Trees grow over years, rivers carve paths slowly, and flowers bloom in their own time. When we rush, we miss the beauty that unfolds naturally. Take time to observe, to listen, and you will see the true magic of the world around you."

Toby listened carefully, feeling a sense of calm wash over him. He realized that in his eagerness to explore, he sometimes overlooked the simple beauty of the forest and the patience it required. He made a promise to himself to slow down, to appreciate the quiet, magical moments that nature offered.

As he stood among the magical creatures, Toby noticed a young fawn watching him shyly from behind the trees. The fawn's fur was soft and spotted, and it had wide, curious eyes. Toby crouched down, extending his hand gently.

The fawn approached slowly, nuzzling his hand as if sensing his respect and kindness. Toby smiled, feeling a deep connection to this gentle creature, understanding that he was a part of this magical place as long as he treated it with care and respect.

After a while, the deer with the crown of flowers spoke again. "Toby, you have shown us that you are willing to listen and learn. The Enchanted Forest is open to you now, and its magic will welcome you whenever you come with a heart full of respect."

Toby bowed again, feeling incredibly honoured. "Thank you. I'll remember everything you've taught me. I'll do my best to care for the forest, wherever I go."

As the sun began to set, casting a golden glow over the clearing, the magical creatures nodded their farewells. The sprites flitted about, leaving trails of sparkling light, the deer and fox retreated into the shadows, and the tortoise gave a slow, wise nod before turning away.

Toby climbed back onto Whistle, feeling a profound sense of peace and gratitude. He looked at his friend, his eyes filled with wonder. "Thank you for bringing me here, Whistle. I feel like I understand so much more about nature and how I can help protect it."

Whistle let out a soft, proud hum. "You have learned well, Toby. Respecting nature is about more than admiration—it's about knowing that we are a part of it and that every choice we make matters. By treating nature with kindness, we allow its magic to thrive."

As they made their way back through the forest, Toby felt a new sense of purpose. He realized that nature was not just a place to explore, but a home to countless creatures, plants, and even unseen magic. He promised himself that he would always remember the lessons he had learned in the Enchanted Forest—to be gentle, to give back, and to be patient.

With Whistle by his side and the wisdom of the forest in his heart, Toby knew he was ready to carry these lessons with him, to be a guardian of the natural world in his own way.

And as they travelled home under the starlit sky, Toby felt that he was part of something much bigger—a magical, interconnected world that thrived on respect, care, and the quiet, powerful beauty of nature.

Chapter 28: Toby's Secret Talent

It was a cool autumn afternoon, and Toby was on his way to Willow Creek Station, feeling both curious and a little uncertain. Recently, he'd watched his friends show off their talents: Leo was great at playing the guitar, and his friend Emma could draw the most incredible pictures. Toby enjoyed cheering them on, but he sometimes wondered if he had any special talents of his own.

As he approached the station, he found Whistle waiting, his headlights casting a warm glow over the platform.

"Hello, Toby," Whistle greeted, sensing the thoughtful look on Toby's face. "Is something on your mind?"

Toby nodded, sitting down beside Whistle. "I've been thinking... I don't know if I have any special talents. All my friends seem to have things they're really good at, but I'm not sure what mine is."

Whistle let out a gentle, reassuring hum. "Ah, but sometimes, Toby, talents are like seeds—they need a little time, patience, and care before they grow and show themselves. Everyone has a unique gift, even if it hasn't been discovered yet."

Toby considered this, feeling a little hopeful. He knew that Whistle was right—talents didn't always appear immediately, and sometimes it took time to figure out what made each person special.

Just then, Whistle let out a cheerful whistle. "I have an idea, Toby. Today, let's go exploring. Sometimes, when we try new things and open ourselves to new experiences, we discover something about ourselves we never knew."

Toby smiled, his curiosity sparking. "Alright, Whistle. Let's go exploring and see what we find!"

With a hum of excitement, Whistle set off along a track that wound through the quieter parts of the forest. They travelled past golden trees, over gently trickling streams, and through fields covered in soft autumn leaves. Toby felt himself relaxing, enjoying the beauty around him as they journeyed further into the woods.

As they moved through a particularly dense part of the forest, they heard a soft, distressed sound nearby. Toby turned, noticing a young rabbit tangled in a patch of brambles, struggling to free itself.

"Oh no! Poor little thing," Toby said, jumping down from Whistle. He moved carefully toward the rabbit, his voice soft and calming. "It's okay. I'll help you."

He knelt down, gently reaching for the brambles to pull them back, being careful not to startle the rabbit. He spoke to it in a gentle voice, telling it not to be afraid. Slowly, he untangled the brambles, making sure not to hurt the rabbit, who seemed to relax at the sound of his voice.

"There you go," Toby said, lifting the last of the brambles away. The rabbit gave him a grateful look, then hopped off into the safety of the bushes.

Whistle watched with admiration. "That was very kind of you, Toby. You have a gentle way with animals, and they seem to trust you easily."

Toby smiled, feeling a small sense of pride. "I've always loved animals, but I never thought it was anything special."

Whistle let out a soft, thoughtful hum. "Kindness and empathy are indeed special gifts, Toby. Not everyone has the patience or calm that you showed with that rabbit. But let's continue our journey and see what else we discover."

They travelled further, and as the day wore on, they came upon a group of birds perched on a tree, chirping loudly as if in distress. Toby noticed that a small bird was tangled in some string that had somehow wound around a branch. The bird was flapping its wings, trying to break free.

"Oh no, another animal in trouble!" Toby said, hurrying over to the tree. He carefully climbed up, moving slowly so as not to frighten the birds, and began to untangle the string. As he worked, he hummed softly, a tune he'd learned from his mom.

The birds seemed to calm down, watching him with interest, and the small bird gradually stopped struggling. Toby freed it from the string, and it flew off, chirping as if to say thank you.

Climbing back down, Toby looked over at Whistle, his face glowing with happiness. "I did it! And I think they understood that I was trying to help."

Whistle's headlights shone warmly. "Toby, you have a natural ability to connect with animals. Your calmness, patience, and empathy are gifts that allow them to feel safe with you. It's a special talent indeed."

Toby's eyes lit up as he thought about this. He'd always felt close to animals and loved spending time with them, but he had never thought of it as a unique skill. Yet today, he had helped two different animals in need, and it had come naturally to him.

Feeling encouraged, Toby decided to experiment a little. He knelt down, calling softly to some squirrels nearby, holding out his hand in a friendly gesture. To his surprise, a curious squirrel cautiously approached him, sniffing his hand before scurrying back to the tree, chittering happily.

Toby looked at Whistle in amazement. "I think you're right! I never realized that animals feel comfortable around me. Maybe that's my talent!"

Whistle let out a pleased hum. "It seems you've found a part of yourself today, Toby. Sometimes, our talents are things that feel so natural to us that we don't even realize they're special. But your ability to connect with animals is truly a gift."

As they made their way back to the station, Toby felt a newfound sense of confidence. He realized that having a talent didn't always mean being able to perform or show off—it could be something as simple and quiet as empathy and kindness. He felt grateful that Whistle had helped him discover this part of himself, something that had been there all along.

When they arrived back at Willow Creek Station, Toby climbed down and placed a gentle hand on Whistle's side. "Thank you for today, Whistle. I feel like I've discovered something important about myself. I may not be able to play an instrument or draw like my friends, but I know I have something special to offer, too."

Whistle gave a warm, approving hum. "Remember, Toby, that every gift, no matter how simple it may seem, has a unique role in the world. Your kindness toward animals shows that you have a gentle spirit, one that others—both people and creatures—will be drawn to. Embrace it, for it's a rare and beautiful talent."

Toby nodded, feeling a sense of pride and purpose he hadn't felt before. He promised himself that he would continue to nurture his connection with animals, using his talent to help them whenever he could.

As he made his way home, Toby felt lighter, carrying with him the joy of discovery. He had learned that talents weren't just about being the best at something—they were about sharing what came naturally, making the world a kinder, better place in whatever way one could.

With a heart full of gratitude and a sense of purpose, Toby walked through the forest, knowing he would always have a special bond with the creatures around him—a bond that was uniquely his. And with Whistle as his guide and friend, he felt ready to embrace this talent and the adventures it would bring.

Chapter 29: The Day of Big Dreams

It was a bright, crisp morning as Toby arrived at Willow Creek Station. Today felt special, though he couldn't quite put his finger on why. The air seemed full of possibility, and Toby felt a gentle excitement in his heart, as if something wonderful was waiting to happen.

When he reached Whistle, his friend's headlights were glowing softly, and Toby sensed that Whistle was in a thoughtful mood.

"Good morning, Whistle," Toby greeted with a smile. "You seem especially peaceful today."

Whistle let out a warm hum. "Good morning, Toby. Today, I thought we could talk about something close to my heart—dreams and the goals we set for ourselves."

Toby's eyes lit up. He'd always enjoyed dreaming about the future and imagining all the adventures that awaited him, but he hadn't really thought about setting goals. "I'd love that, Whistle. I think about all kinds of dreams, but I'm not sure how to make them happen."

Whistle chuckled gently. "Well, dreams are like stars, Toby. They're bright and inspiring, something to reach for. But to get to them, we often need a path—a set of steps that bring us closer bit by bit. That's where goals come in."

Toby thought about this as he climbed onto the platform, settling into his usual spot beside Whistle. "So goals are like... the little steps that help us reach our big dreams?"

"Exactly," Whistle replied. "Everyone has dreams, Toby. But it's those who take the time to set goals who turn their dreams into reality. Goals are what keep us focused, even when the journey is long or challenging."

As they travelled along the familiar tracks through the forest, Whistle continued. "Let me share one of my dreams with you. Ever since I found my voice and became a magical train, I've dreamed of guiding Listeners like you. I want to teach them about kindness, courage, and the magic of the world around them."

Toby looked up, feeling a warmth in his chest. "That's a beautiful dream, Whistle. And you're already doing it!"

Whistle let out a soft, grateful hum. "Yes, but it didn't happen all at once. I had to be patient, learning to communicate, to listen, and to understand the needs of those I guide. Each Listener I meet brings me closer to that dream, just as you do, Toby."

Toby nodded, feeling inspired by Whistle's story. He realized that big dreams often took time and effort to grow, and that each step mattered.

After a while, Whistle asked, "What about you, Toby? Do you have any dreams for the future?"

Toby thought carefully, letting his imagination wander. "I do! I dream of exploring more magical places, learning everything I can about the forest, and maybe even helping others understand the beauty of nature. I want to make a difference, like you, Whistle."

"That's a wonderful dream," Whistle said warmly. "Now, think about what small goals could help you get there. What steps could you take today, or this week, to bring you closer to your dream?"

Toby considered this, feeling a surge of excitement. "I could start by learning more about nature and the creatures in the forest. Maybe I could study different plants and animals so I understand them better. And I could also try sharing what I learn with my friends."

Whistle gave a pleased hum. "Those are excellent goals, Toby. By setting small, achievable steps, you'll find yourself moving steadily toward your dream. And as you go, each goal you accomplish will help you build confidence and keep you inspired."

As they continued their journey, Toby felt the excitement of having a plan. He realized that setting goals didn't mean giving up on big dreams—it meant finding a way to bring those dreams into the present, one step at a time.

After a moment, he asked, "Do you think dreams ever change, Whistle?"

Whistle let out a thoughtful hum. "Yes, Toby. Sometimes, as we grow and learn, our dreams evolve. We discover new interests or new ways to make a difference. Changing dreams isn't a failure—it's a sign that we're paying attention to our hearts and minds."

Toby smiled, feeling reassured. "So it's okay if my dreams grow and change, as long as I keep setting goals and working toward what feels right?"

"Exactly," Whistle replied. "Every dream, whether big or small, is part of the journey. And each goal helps us learn more about who we are and what we're capable of."

They travelled through the forest, talking about their dreams and the ways they could make them happen. Toby felt a new sense of purpose, knowing that he didn't have to achieve everything all at once. His dreams were like stars in the sky, guiding him, and his goals were the steps that would help him reach them.

As they returned to Willow Creek Station, Toby looked up at Whistle with gratitude. "Thank you for helping me understand, Whistle. I feel like my dreams are closer now, even though I have a long way to go."

Whistle gave a gentle, encouraging hum. "Remember, Toby, that each step forward, no matter how small, brings you closer to your dreams. And with patience, persistence, and belief in yourself, you'll see those dreams take shape."

With a newfound sense of purpose, Toby waved goodbye and headed home, his mind buzzing with ideas for his goals. He knew that he was on a path that would bring him closer to his dreams, and that each small step he took would help him grow, learn, and make a difference.

As he walked through the forest, Toby felt inspired and hopeful, ready to embrace each goal, each challenge, and every wonderful step on the journey toward his big dreams.

Chapter 30: One Last Ride

The day had finally come, the day Toby had known was approaching but had hoped might never arrive. Today, he and Whistle would take one final journey together before Whistle left for his next adventure. The sky was a brilliant blue, with soft clouds drifting lazily, and the forest around Willow Creek Station seemed alive with a quiet, bittersweet magic.

When Toby arrived at the station, he found Whistle waiting for him, headlights glowing gently, as if filled with their shared memories. Toby took a deep breath, knowing that this last ride would be something he would cherish forever.

"Hello, Whistle," Toby said softly, his voice carrying both excitement and sadness.

"Hello, Toby," Whistle replied warmly, sensing the weight of the moment. "Are you ready for one last adventure?"

Toby nodded, a small smile breaking through his sadness. "Yes, I am. Let's make it the best one yet."

With a gentle hum, Whistle began to move along the tracks, carrying them through the familiar forest. They passed the winding paths and tall trees that had been witnesses to countless adventures. Each bend in the track seemed to hold memories of lessons learned, of laughter shared, of discoveries made side by side.

As they travelled, Whistle spoke softly, his voice filled with warmth and gratitude. "Toby, this journey is as much about our memories as it is about saying goodbye. I want you to remember every place we pass, every lesson you've learned. They're a part of you now, as you are a part of me."

Toby listened, taking in every word, feeling the memories flow through him like the tracks beneath Whistle. He remembered the first day he'd found the hidden station, the thrill of discovering Whistle and the magic that lived within him. He remembered each adventure, each friendship they'd made, and each lesson that had helped him grow.

They passed the clearing where they'd met the wise owl, Eldric, who had taught Toby about wisdom and making wise choices. Toby smiled, waving to the trees as if Eldric were still watching over him. Then they passed the stream where he had helped the injured bird, a reminder of kindness and empathy.

"Do you remember, Toby," Whistle said softly, "how you once felt unsure of your own talents? And now, look at all the ways you've discovered who you are."

Toby nodded, feeling a mixture of pride and gratitude. "I remember. You helped me see that I could make a difference, Whistle. I never thought I had anything special to offer, but now I know that everyone has something unique to share."

They travelled onward, reaching the hidden valley where wishes came true, the enchanted forest where he'd met magical creatures who taught him about respecting nature, and the narrow, winding tracks through the mountain where he'd faced his fears. Each place held its own magic, its own story, and Toby felt his heart fill with the richness of these memories.

After a while, Whistle brought them to a gentle stop on a hilltop overlooking the entire forest. The view was breathtaking, with the golden sunlight streaming through the trees, casting a warm glow over the landscape. Toby felt as though he could see every place they had been, every moment they had shared, all stretching out before him like a map of their friendship.

They sat in silence, taking in the beauty of the scene, both knowing that this was a perfect moment to hold in their hearts forever.

"Toby," Whistle began, his voice soft but strong, "this journey has been as meaningful to me as it has been to you. You've shown me that friendships, even those that change, never truly end. They live on in our hearts, guiding us wherever we go."

Toby felt tears prick his eyes, but they were tears of gratitude more than sadness. He looked up at Whistle, his voice filled with love. "Thank you, Whistle. You've been my best friend, my teacher, my guide. I'll never forget everything you've shown me. And I promise, I'll keep making a difference, just like you taught me."

They stayed there for a while, the quietness of the forest wrapping around them like a warm embrace. Toby felt as though he were saying goodbye not just to Whistle, but to a part of himself—a part that would always stay with him, woven into every step he took from here on.

Finally, as the sun began to dip toward the horizon, casting a golden light over the forest, Whistle gently turned back toward Willow Creek Station. Toby knew the journey was ending, but he also knew that this was a goodbye filled with love, with meaning, and with the promise of all the memories they'd shared.

As they arrived back at the station, Toby climbed down from Whistle for the last time, his heart full and heavy all at once. He placed his hand gently on Whistle's side, feeling the warmth of their connection one final time.

"Goodbye, Whistle," Toby said softly, his voice steady. "Thank you for everything."

Whistle's headlights glowed brightly, and his voice was filled with pride and love. "Goodbye, Toby. You are ready for your own journey now. Remember that I'll always be with you, in every lesson, every memory, and every act of kindness you share."

With a final, heartfelt hum, Whistle slowly began to pull away, his wheels turning as he set off down the tracks. Toby watched, waving until Whistle was just a glimmer in the distance, the soft sound of his whistle echoing through the trees one last time.

As Toby stood in the quiet of the station, he felt the warmth of Whistle's presence settle deep within his heart. Though his friend was no longer beside him, Toby knew that he was carrying Whistle's lessons with him, guiding him as he set off on his own path.

With a final look at the tracks, Toby took a deep breath, turning toward the forest, ready to continue his journey. He knew that Whistle would always be a part of him, a voice in his heart that would light the way forward.

And so, with a heart full of gratitude, memories, and the promise of all that lay ahead, Toby stepped into his future, carrying the gift of his friendship with Whistle—a gift that would stay with him, wherever the journey took him.

Chapter 31: Passing It On

Years had passed since that last ride with Whistle. Toby was no longer the young boy who'd stumbled upon the hidden train station; he was now a grown man with a family of his own. But even after all this time, the memory of Whistle remained vivid in his heart, like a bright light guiding him through life's many adventures.

One crisp autumn afternoon, Toby found himself standing once more at the edge of Willow Creek Station. He hadn't been here in years, but everything felt so familiar—the soft rustling of leaves, the gentle whisper of the forest. And though Whistle was no longer there, Toby could feel his presence as if his old friend were right beside him.

Beside him stood his two young children, a boy and a girl, wide-eyed and curious as they looked around. They had heard snippets of their father's stories—tales of talking trains, magical creatures, enchanted forests, and lessons of kindness and courage. But today, Toby had brought them here to share the full story of Whistle, the magical train who had been his greatest friend and teacher.

"Daddy," his son asked, looking up at him with bright eyes, "is this the place where you met Whistle?"

Toby smiled, feeling a wave of warmth as he knelt down beside his children. "Yes, it is," he said gently. "This is where it all began. I found this station by accident when I was about your age, and that's when I met Whistle. He was the one who taught me so many things—about kindness, courage, and the magic that exists in the world if you know where to look."

His daughter's eyes sparkled with wonder. "Did Whistle really talk, Daddy? And did you really go on adventures together?"

Toby nodded, smiling at the excitement in their eyes. "He did. Whistle was unlike any friend I'd ever had. He could talk, he had wisdom beyond any I'd known, and he guided me through so many amazing adventures. Together, we met wise animals, explored hidden places, and even learned how to face our fears."

The children listened, captivated by each word, as Toby told them stories of the magical valley of wishes, the wise owl Eldric, the enchanted forest, and all the creatures and lessons he and Whistle had encountered. He shared the story of their final journey together, explaining how Whistle had to leave to guide new friends, but that his friendship and lessons had stayed with him.

When he finished, his son looked thoughtful. "Do you think Whistle is still out there somewhere, helping someone else?"

Toby smiled, feeling a deep sense of peace. "I do. Whistle was meant to guide those who need him, just like he guided me. And though we had to say goodbye, his spirit, his kindness, and everything he taught me—those things live on. I think, in a way, Whistle is with all of us, in every act of kindness we share and every adventure we take."

His daughter looked around, as if hoping to catch a glimpse of Whistle in the distance. "Do you think we'll ever see him?"

"Maybe not in the way I did," Toby replied, "but Whistle lives on through the stories we share. When we pass on the lessons of kindness, courage, and respect for the world around us, we're keeping his spirit alive. And maybe, one day, if you listen carefully, you might hear a whistle in the distance or feel his warmth in a moment of kindness. That's Whistle, reminding us that he's still with us."

The children looked up at him, a sense of awe in their eyes as they realized that they, too, were part of Whistle's story now.

"Will you tell us the stories again, Daddy?" his son asked, his voice full of hope.

Toby chuckled softly, pulling his children close. "I will. And one day, when you're grown, you can pass the stories on to your own children, just like I'm passing them to you. That's how Whistle's legacy lives on—through each of us, through each act of kindness, each lesson, and each story we tell."

As they sat together at Willow Creek Station, Toby felt a quiet joy. He knew that Whistle would always be with them, woven into the fabric of their family, passed down through generations as a reminder of the magic of friendship and the power of kindness.

And as they stood to leave, Toby thought he heard a faint, familiar whistle echo through the trees, as if Whistle were watching over them still, his spirit carried forward in every story, every memory, and every new adventure yet to come.

Disclaimer:

This book is a work of fiction. All characters, events, and locations described within are entirely imaginary or used in a fictitious manner. Any resemblance to actual persons, living or deceased, or real locations and events is purely coincidental.

The adventures in this book are intended to spark imagination and wonder. While Toby and Whistle explore forests, old train tracks, and hidden places, readers are reminded that exploring unknown areas can be dangerous and should always be done with the guidance of an adult.

This story is meant to entertain and inspire young minds, encouraging them to cherish friendships, embrace curiosity, and find adventure in safe and responsible ways.

Milton Keynes UK
Ingram Content Group UK Ltd.
UKHW030851111124
451035UK00001B/151